THE UNTHINKABLE HYBRID

THE UNTHINKABLE HYBRID

Book - 1

THE DARK SIDE OF PARADISE

By

V.F. Wyler

Lone Dragon Press

Illinois

This book is for Hannah Walker and her mom, Julie, who provided inspiration, photographs and, most of all, faith. Thanks, ladies!

The Unthinkable Hybrid Book 1 – The Dark Side of Paradise

Copyright © 2008 – 2017 by V.F. Wyler and James D. Thompson

Published by Lone Dragon Press

Library of Congress Catalog Card Number: Pending

ISBN: 978-0692920145

Printed in the USA

Prologue

March, 1956. The full moon shone brightly over the Project Omega test facility, drenching the compound, and the lonely expanse of Nevada desert land that surrounded it, in silvery incandescence.

Save for the grim-faced Marine guards that patrolled inside the fence, and the two that stood like a pair of granite statues outside the main gate, there were no signs of life at the compound. Only Top Brass and political and scientific bigwigs were allowed anywhere near Project Omega, with only one exception – and that had been a strange and single occurrence.

The older of the two guards outside the gate pulled a wrinkled pack of cigarettes from his shirt pocket as he recalled that peculiar incident and offered one to the younger guard standing beside him.

"Care for a smoke?"

"Thanks, sarge," the younger Marine said as he gratefully took the cigarette and put it to his lips. "It's cold out here tonight."

"The desert's cold every night," the sergeant observed. He fished in his pocket for his Zippo. "It gets into a man's bones after a while." When he found the lighter, he lit both cigarettes and then glanced around at the sand-strewn wasteland that skirted the compound.

The sergeant had been stationed at the test facility for over a year, and now that his hitch was up, he was happy he would be posted elsewhere. He'd hated this assignment. He knew that the compound housed some awful secret and had no desire to be around when that secret, whatever terrible thing it was, finally came to light.

"Yeah, I hate this desert," the young Marine confessed. "Hotter than blue-blazes during the day, colder than a well digger's foot at night, and full of sounds..." He looked over the barren rocks that loomed west of the gate. "Queer sounds," he went on, "like moans and echoes and wails..." He shuddered. "It makes your blood run cold when you think about it."

"That's only the wind," the sergeant replied in his gravelly voice. "There's nothing out there to be scared of." He gestured back at the test facility. "It's what's going on *in there* that should scare you." He looked grim. "There's nothing healthy going on in there. I'd stake my last dime on that."

The younger man took a drag off his cigarette and nodded. "Yeah," he said. "I think you're onto something there, sarge."

"You bet I am," the sergeant replied. "That egg-headed Kraut is up to something. Something *nobody* ought to be doing." He glanced back once more at the darkened compound for emphasis. "And mark my words, Sanders… one of these days it's gonna blow up in his face! I just hope I'm out of here before it does."

The young Marine looked over at the sergeant curiously. "How about them suits that came in here last week?" he asked. "And whatever happened to that kid the Kraut had us bring in here last summer? I ain't seen him since the day we lugged him into the infirmary."

The sergeant shook his head gravely. "If you're smart, you won't worry about it," he warned. "And don't mention that to anyone. Like I told you before, that's classified." He threw down his half-burned cigarette and stamped it out under a booted foot. "Besides, some things a man had ought to leave alone. And that's one of them."

Before the younger man could form a reply, both men were startled by the sound of an explosion behind them. After exchanging a swift, shocked glance, the two men whirled around to try and make out what had happened. The alarm bell was ringing inside the facility building, and there was a cloud of smoke pouring from a large hole in the west face of the compound. A cadre´ of their fellow Marines were milling around inside the fence, barking and acknowledging orders, their weapons drawn and held at the ready

"What the hell was *that*?" the young Marine shouted over the din.

The sergeant un-slung his Thompson submachine gun and held it ready. "Nothing good, you can bet on that!"

At first, the sergeant assumed that one of the scientists had mixed a bad batch of chemicals, which had exploded. He was soon to discover that he was wrong, however. As the cloud of smoke pouring from the hole in the side of the building gradually dissipated, the sergeant could make out a pair of small, yellow lights moving through the haze, and with them, a hulking shape nearly seven feet tall. It waived simian long arms to bat away the remaining smoke. As the shape drew nearer, the sergeant began to wonder whether he was having a nightmare.

"What is it, sarge?" the young Marine stammered as he raised his M1 Garand.

But, the older man didn't answer. How could he? He had never seen anything like the brute that advanced on them through the haze. The thing was hard to make out with all the smoke, but it appeared to have the general build of a mountain gorilla – huge and powerful, with eyes that seemed to glow like twin lanterns.

There were shouts and calls of fright from the Marines still inside the fence as the thing advanced on the gate, waiving its long arms and bellowing angrily. Gunshots rang out and muzzle flashes lit up the grounds. A few Marines charged the marauder and were flung away like children. Screams of horror and pain joined the turmoil while the alarm bell rang on incessantly in the background.

"Get ready!" the sergeant shouted as the beast neared the electrified gate. He aimed his machine gun, his duty and training holding him to his spot, in spite of his better judgment.

Beside the sergeant, his young compatriot was far less confident. He aimed his rifle, but his arms were trembling and his knees knocking.

The monster, for no other term could adequately describe such a creature, thundered on toward the gate, batting away smoke, bullets and attacking Marines with equal ease. It was a juggernaut – an unstoppable force, and it seemed determined to escape the compound. At last, it reached the electrified gate and stretched out great clawed hands to seize it.

"Let him have it!" the sergeant shouted, and unleashed a hail of bullets from his Thompson. His companion followed suit and soon, the oncoming horror was met with an unceasing barrage of gunfire as it attacked the gate.

But, the bullets were useless! The two Marines could hear them twang as they ricocheted off of the monster's iron-hard body like pebbles thrown against a brick wall.

The monster bellowed in rage and seized the electrified gate with both huge hands. A blinding shower of sparks erupted from the gate as more than 3,000 volts of electricity shuddered over the snarling brute's hulking body. It ripped the gate from its brick moorings, crumpled it into a sizzling ball, and hurled it aside like a wad of used tinfoil.

Goggle-eyed, the young Marine tossed away his useless rifle and dove aside to avoid the unyielding beast's great, flaying claws.

The older Marine, however, a grizzled veteran of both World War II and Korea, was too well-trained to throw in the towel so easily. When his Thompson went dry, he raised it like a club and charged the gruesome behemoth, determined to assail the thing with the butt of his weapon.

The monster, however, was weary of these feeble attacks and sent the older Marine spinning senseless to the ground with a single swat of his huge paw.

The young Marine rose up from where he'd thrown himself and stared after the retreating goliath with unbelieving eyes. He watched, slack-jawed, as the behemoth let out one final bellow, then tromped off into the night-shrouded desert, steam still rising from its steely body.

As the nightmare finally disappeared over the lonely hills, the young Marine was vaguely aware of the alarm bell still sounding in the compound behind him, and of the shouts and clamor of his fellow Marines. But, it all seemed to be happening to someone else – like in a dream. By the time his compatriots reached him, the young Marine had slumped to the ground in a dead faint.

Chapter-1

June, 1956. A pair of headlights broke the gloom on the lonely length of rural blacktop stretching between the small southern California towns of San Mateo and Maplewood. After a moment, a red, 1955 Chevrolet Bel Air came around a bend in the winding road and trundled along at a leisurely pace.

Driving the car was sixteen-year-old Betty Jo Carlson, a striking girl with eyes as blue as the sea, and golden hair that was neatly curled and done up in a ponytail with a soft, pink ribbon.

Seated next to Betty Jo was her seven-year-old brother, Johnny, a chubby-cheeked cherub of a boy who strongly resembled his older sister, but in a tousled, less civilized way. In his striped tee-shirt and dungarees, his hair affably mussed, Johnny made up for his sister's impeccable tidiness and refined teenage beauty with a general, yet endearing sloppiness.

For Johnny, it had been a capitol evening. After much goading, he'd conned his older sibling into taking him to the drive-in in San Mateo to see *The Mutants of Mars,* the latest in the seemingly endless string of grade-B science fiction efforts from the cesspools of Hollywood. Johnny, of course, had been dazzled by the film and was still waving his toy rocket ship back and forth in the seat beside Betty Jo, pretending they were in mid-flight to the red planet.

For her own part, Betty Jo felt she'd just wasted a dollar, to say nothing of a perfectly good Saturday night. On top of that, she'd had to turn down a date with Tommy Fisher, the handsome captain of the high school debating team, in order to placate her little brother. Other girls her age would have rankled over such a situation, but not Betty Jo. She couldn't afford to.

When her mother passed away four years earlier, Betty Jo was forced to get along with her little brother in a way unheard of for most siblings. She was now not only Johnny's older sister, but his surrogate mother as well, a fact that had matured the blonde beauty well beyond her sixteen years. Her father, Dr. David Carlson, had also come to rely heavily on his daughter. With such grave responsibilities to ground her, Betty Jo was usually above petty teenage angst.

In spite of her admirable self-control, however, Betty Jo was still flustered over the current state of affairs. Her father had left the day before to attend an academic conference in Sacramento and wouldn't be home until Sunday night. This meant that Betty Jo had no choice but to spend the whole weekend babysitting her kid brother.

She wasn't about to drag the often unruly whelp along on one of her dates, especially not a date with Tommy Fisher. This left the teenager with little alternative than to indulge the child and take him to the movies. The result – an evening spent watching a bad monster movie and flicking popcorn kernels off of her expensive, pink sweater. Betty Jo sighed heavily as she drove. She'd had worse evenings, but not many.

Beside her, Johnny was busy making rocket noises and barking out arbitrary orders from Mission Control in the deepest, most authoritative voice he could muster.

Finally, Betty Jo grew weary of his constant prattle and glanced irritably at her little brother. "Settle down, will you, Buck Rogers?" she commanded. "One more order from Mission Control and I'm going to mutiny!"

Johnny grinned up at his older sister. "Wasn't that a swell movie, sis?" he chirped.

Betty Jo rolled her eyes. "Oh, sure," she replied snidely. "Best movie I've ever seen."

"Just about," Johnny agreed, missing the sarcasm in his sister's remark. He looked up at Betty Jo with sparkling, blue eyes. "Aren't you glad we came?"

Betty Jo glanced over at her little brother, amused that he could be so easily impressed. She smiled and roughed his tousled, blonde mop. "I suppose so."

After a moment, Johnny looked thoughtfully at his toy rocket ship, "Gee," he mused, "I wonder if we'll ever really be able to fly in space?"

Betty Jo shrugged, only half listening. "Perhaps," she commented. "But, if we do, it won't be for several years yet."

Johnny's brow furrowed. "Golly," he lamented, "I was hoping it'd be sooner than that."

Betty Jo smiled blandly. "Why?" she asked. "You won't be going."

Johnny puffed out his chest, offended. "Who says I won't be going?" he demanded.

His older sister grinned. "I believe you have to be out of grammar school to join the Space Program."

Johnny opened his mouth to object, but then shifted gears abruptly. "Hey, sis," he asked, "do you suppose there really are monsters on Mars?"

Betty Jo shook her head. "Don't be silly, Johnny," she admonished. "There are no such things as monsters, on Mars, or any place else. Those silly movies are all just..." She broke off suddenly as she noticed something in the middle of the road ahead of them.

"Just *what*?" Johnny prodded.

Betty Jo ignored him. She narrowed her blue eyes and stared ahead, trying to ascertain what it was that was plodding along the blacktop before them. Whatever it was, it was large. A deer, perhaps? But, no – the shape was wrong. It could be a bear, she told herself, but dispelled that idea quickly, too. Bears had long ago vanished from Corman County.

As the Bel Air bore down on the mysterious object, its shape became more distinct. It looked like a huge, upright gorilla lumbering right in the middle of the road. Betty Jo peered over the steering wheel, a sense of dread welling up inside her. It couldn't be a gorilla. But, what could it be, then?

Johnny noticed the growing look of alarm forming on his sister's exquisite features. "What is it, Jo-Jo?" he demanded.

But, his sister couldn't answer. The thing on the road ahead of them had noticed the Bel Air's headlamps bearing down on it, and had turned around to face the oncoming vehicle. Now, its whole, monstrous form was caught in the glare of the sealed beams and quite visible. Betty Jo couldn't believe her eyes. They flew wide and a scream caught in her throat and lodged there, forming a stifling lump.

"Sis?" Johnny yelped excitedly. "What's the matter?"

Betty Jo's mouth opened, but only a tiny squeak escaped.

The thing on the road threw up huge, scaly paws to shield its catlike, yellow eyes from the glare of the headlamps. It was an impossible thing – a merger of ape and crocodile, and it wore what looked like the tattered remnants of a radiation suit. It was, for lack of a better word, a *monster*!

Johnny saw the horror etched on Betty Jo's lovely face and he looked out of the windshield to see what had frightened his older sister. He was sorry he did. "Turn, Betty Jo!" he shouted as the car bore down on the hideous apparition. *"Turn!"*

At last, the beautiful teenager found voice. She let out a shrill scream and jerked the steering wheel violently to the right, narrowly missing the hulking brute that still stood like an iron statue in the middle of the road.

But, to her horror, Betty Jo saw, too late, that she had over-steered. The Bel Air crashed through the white, wooden guardrail at the side of the road and plummeted down the steep embankment of the gully beyond. Inside the car, the two terrified Carlson siblings were buffeted wildly about, eventually banging their heads sharply together and plunging suddenly into unconsciousness.

The Chevy, now pilotless and wholly out-of-control, rumbled on down the bank and smashed into a large oak tree at the bottom of the gully. Almost immediately, flames began to flicker under the crumpled hood and, in a matter of a few seconds, spread, thanks to the dried grass common in the gully, until the whole car was surrounded by a wicked, dancing fire.

On the roadside above, the mutant goliath stood, staring down at the wrecked car in the gully, and the rising flames that grew up around it, threatening to swallow both the car, and its helpless occupants. The monster paced along the road's edge, growing more uneasy by the second. Somewhere in the dark, hazy mists of his primitive brain, the remnants of a memory began to surface – a memory of smoke and fire and of the screams of those in peril, those he had loved.

But, that memory was an old one – before the *Bad Place.* Now, it was merely a blur in the behemoth's vague brain – a hazy dreamlike image, shrouded in mystery. He could not remember who those people in the other car had been, nor could he remember why he'd been unable to help them. But, he could remember the car itself, surrounded by deadly flames, just like the car in the gully below. He also recalled the pain and loss that accompanied those images.

The beast ceased his agitated pacing, then, and came to a decision. The little ones trapped in the burning car below would not perish in the flames as the others had done. The others he could not help, but these two he *could* help. This time he had the *power*!

With a shriek of rage, the atom-spawned giant thundered down the bank into the fire-filled gully below, ignoring the fearsome heat and suffocating smoke. For a man, the wall of flames that surrounded the wrecked Bel Air was an impenetrable barrier of seething doom, hissing and crackling, as the dried grass and shrubbery in the gully were consumed by the ravenous fire.

But the beast was not a man. He was something less, but also much more. His huge body, forged by chemicals and isotopes into a walking fortress, was all but indestructible. Without fear and feeling no pain, the steely leviathan rumbled right through the vicious flames. Within seconds, he was standing beside the ruined car. He searched inside the wreck with his fiery, feline eyes and located the two unconscious children in short order. They were slumped together in the front seat, their golden hair mussed, neither one moving.

The mutant behemoth seized the roof of the Chevy and peeled it back like the lid of a sardine can. He snatched up the crumpled driver's side door and tossed it away. Then, he leaned into the car to retrieve the two fragile occupants.

It proved difficult for him to wriggle his great, clawed paw beneath the limp girl, but he did so carefully, and then rested her soft body against his vast, iron-hard chest. He then reached for the boy. He scooped the child up quickly and settled him on his chest alongside the girl. Then, with both children cradled against his huge body, shielded by his long, bulging arms, the monster started back up the embankment, doing his best to dodge the worst patches of fire along the way.

It didn't take the creature long to lope up the embankment. When he reached the top, he carefully laid the two children in the yellowed grass growing along the road's edge and crouched over them protectively. The move was instinctive, not thoughtful, but fortunate all the same, for, almost at that very moment, the gas tank of the fire besieged Bel Air heated up and exploded violently, showering down red-hot shards of debris for three hundred feet or more.

The monster bent over the two Carlson kids, shielding their delicate bodies from the fiery barrage until the flaming fragments ceased to shudder down from the billowing cloud of smoke churning up from the hellish gully.

After a moment, the beast threw a look over his broad shoulder and saw that the fire was dying down, as the car and most of the dried foliage in the arid gully had, by now, been consumed. When he was sure it was safe to do so, the brute rose up on his haunches and gazed down at the two fragile beings he had rescued.

16

The girl, with her golden hair in gentle curls and her round face only slightly smudged, was beautiful. The little boy, his head resting just beneath the girl's ample bosom, was tousled and smudged, but seemed otherwise unharmed. Neither the boy, nor the girl moved or made a sound. Had their ordeal put them, somehow, into this listless state? Were they asleep, or worse – dead? The monster was concerned as he peered down at them. Had all his efforts to save them from their fiery fate been in vain? He couldn't tell.

The beast leaned down and sniffed the boy, then nudged his cheek with his leathery, whiskered muzzle. He noticed the boy stir slightly and saw the child's little pug nose wrinkle. It was a great relief to the worried goliath.

He then turned his attention to the girl. He first sniffed her pretty face, and was pleased by her sweet, flowery scent – a scent that lingered on her in spite of the corrupting smell of smoke that hung over everything. He sniffed her again, and this time, the girl moved, her plump lips parted and she drew in a deep breath. Her breast swelled, then rose and fell rhythmically. The monster hovered over her, anxious for her to come to.

Slowly, painfully, the fog began to clear from Betty Jo's mind. When it did, a terrible, throbbing pain shot through her head. She moaned and reached up a hand to inspect her injured scalp. With her eyes still squeezed shut, she located the stinging knot on the right side of her head, and the raw, bloody spot at its center. She had obviously been knocked unconscious.

Thinking was made nearly impossible by the endless pounding coursing through her skull. She couldn't yet process what had happened to her. She recalled that it had something to do with the car. Where was Johnny? The thought of her little brother in peril sobered the woozy teenager and her whirling thoughts began slowly to coalesce. Gradually, her blue eyes opened.

At first, the images that leaked into her mind were blurry and hazy. Betty Jo reached up a hand and rubbed her eyes, then looked again. Something was hovering over her, still unclear, however. She closed her eyes again and concentrated. Her thoughts were stabilizing by now, despite the pain, and she remembered going through the guardrail and trundling down into the gully. She'd obviously hit her head along the way, for she didn't recall crashing the car.

She could feel a weight on top of her and reached down to feel a soft cheek and mussed hair perched atop her breast. Johnny, she realized. But, who was it hovering over her?

The acrid scents of smoke and burnt rubber were now beginning to filter into her senses. Had some passerby spotted the wreck and come to their aid? Yes, that had to be it. How else could they have escaped the car? Betty Jo struggled to focus her blurry eyes. She peered up at the hulking shape still hovering over her.

Slowly, her sight cleared and the monstrous image came into focus.

It was an image straight out of a nightmare – the face of a gorilla and a crocodile, impossibly merged into a single horrid visage. It stared down at her with the fiery yellow eyes of a cat and sniffed her with a blue-black, leathery muzzle that was lined with a tiger's prominent whiskers. Atop its head, jutting out from amid a black, tangled, horse-like mane, were two wolfish, pointed ears that twitched with every sound, as a dog's might.

The thing grunted curiously. It was the same horror Betty Jo had seen standing in the road earlier, the thing that had caused her to wreck in the first place! Now it loomed over her, like a demon out of a bad dream, come, perhaps, to claim her from the flames. As the horrid beast thrust its ugly, whiskered muzzle toward her, Betty Jo let out a horrified shriek and slumped back to the ground, her mind swirling once more into a quagmire of darkness.

The monster groaned, disappointed. The girl had come to for a moment and then passed out again. On top of that, she had screamed again – screamed as if she were terrified. Why? She was no longer in danger. She and the little boy were both quite safe from the fire. What was it that had frightened her? The mutant behemoth nudged the girl's soft cheek, puzzled and a little hurt.

He had hoped to make friends with these two little golden creatures. He had no other friends, save for the old man. But the girl, at least, seemed to be afraid of him, just like every other human the beast had encountered. Only the old man showed no fear of him.

Thinking of the old man gave the monster a plan. If he took the two children to him, the old man might be able to wake them up and help them. The old man was wise in such things. He might also teach them not to be afraid of the monster, and that seemed like a good idea to the beast.

He stood up slowly and was about to reach for the boy when he noticed another pair of lights coming up the road toward them and heard the roar of another car engine. His pointed ears perked up in a fright.

Just up the road, the other car, a sharp looking Model-A hotrod known to most of the residents of Corman County as the *Purple Bomb*, roared down the grade. The driver of the car was a plump, freckle-faced boy of seventeen named Eugene Walters Jr., but everyone just called him "Skip". Skip had made up for his plumpness and lack of athletic prowess by, over the course of two long years, gradually building the mighty Purple Bomb. Although he still wasn't terribly popular among either the boys, or the girls at Maplewood High school, owning the Bomb, at least, had earned him a certain grudging degree of respect.

Tonight, Skip had taken the Bomb out on a test run to San Mateo after giving her a thorough tune-up, and was on his way back along Brush Canyon Road. He'd opened her up, and the Bomb's powerful engine screamed as Skip negotiated the perilous curves along the winding stretch of rural blacktop.

Just as Skip was thinking he'd better slow down for fear of running across the Sheriff, or one of his deputies, out patrolling the canyon road, the boy spotted a huge cloud of black smoke billowing up out of the gully ahead. He raised an eyebrow, curious. Even a mile distant, he could smell the acrid stink of burnt rubber wafting on the cool night breeze.

"Yikes!" the fat teenager remarked to himself. "Looks like somebody had a pile-up down in the gully. Hope nobody was killed."

Skip stepped on the gas pedal and felt the hotrod lurch forward. As he rounded the bend in the road just ahead of the gully, he could see that the fire was already dying down. Apparently, the worst was over. But that was small comfort when someone might be lying dead down in the gully. The thought gave Skip a shudder.

Also, a fire of any size was a dangerous thing in an arid region. It could easily get out of control and spread. Wildfires were a constant menace in southern California. Whatever else might have happened in the gully, Skip realized he'd have to alert the fire department straight away.

As he neared the gully, and the column of smoke still jutting up from it, Skip spotted two small, pastel figures lying prone in the yellowed grass by the roadside near a gap in the white, wooden guardrail. It was obvious to the boy that these figures had to be the occupants of the car that burned in the gully. Clearly, they had been thrown out of the wreck, probably when their car hit the guardrail.

But then, Skip noticed a third figure standing over the two who were lying in the grass by the road – a hulking, grayish figure that looked, for all the world, to be a gorilla!

Skip rubbed his eyes and when he looked again, the apelike monstrosity had vanished. Had it really been there at all, or had the flickering light from the dying fire in the gully merely played tricks on his weary eyes? It had been, after all, a long and tiring day for Skip.

He decided it was best not to dwell on the notion. Skip was not known for his courage, and the thought of a gorilla roaming loose in the lonely, desert hills of Brush Canyon was enough to send shivers down his spine.

Skip pulled the Purple Bomb to the side of the road near the two prone figures and parked her, but he kept the motor running – just in case. When he got out of the car, Skip saw at once that the unconscious figures in the grass were Betty Jo and Johnny Carlson, his next-door-neighbors.

"Holy cow!" the plump boy stammered. "It's Jo and Johnny!" He glanced past the damaged guardrail down the embankment at the plume of smoke and flickering flames below. "Then, that has to be Jo's Chevy burning up down there."

Skip hurried to where the two Carlsons were lying, rolled Johnny gently aside, and scooped Betty Jo carefully into his pudgy arms. As he lifted her, Skip felt his heart fluttering. More than any girl he'd ever known, Skip loved the beautiful, blonde Betty Jo. She had been his deepest crush since the first day she and her family moved next door to him four years before, though he dared not confess his love.

Betty Jo was an icon in Maplewood social circles, a golden goddess beyond the reach of mere mortals like Skip. As such, he'd been forced to admire her from afar – well, from over the wooden fence that separated their two yards, at any rate. Now, even with his love unrequited, Skip would have happily given away his prized Purple Bomb if it meant the girl of his dreams was not badly injured.

Once he had Betty Jo safely placed in the seat of his hotrod, Skip returned and hoisted Johnny. Skip was much less fond of the bratty, sharp tongued seven-year-old than he was of the boy's comely sister, but he also knew how fond Betty Jo was of her peevish kid brother, and how badly she would feel if any harm came to the little blonde imp. Keeping that in mind, Skip was as gentle as possible as he settled Johnny in the seat next to his sister.

With his two passengers safely aboard, Skip climbed into the driver's seat and revved up the Purple Bomb's mighty engine. A split second later, they were roaring away from the gully down the canyon road. As he drove, Skip glanced nervously at his two unconscious charges.

"They look pretty banged-up," he told himself. "The hospital in San Bolero is too far, and old Doc Lawson is out of town..." Skip pondered a moment, trying to think of alternatives. Then, he remembered the old British professor who had recently bought the run-down farmhouse at the edge of Brush Canyon. He lived less than a mile away. Skip had heard that, among other things, the eccentric old gentleman was a doctor.

Skip made up his mind. He would take Betty Jo and Johnny to this kook of an old man and hope the old fellow wasn't as much of a crank as the gossip mongers of Maplewood made him out to be.

As the powerful Purple Bomb sped away and disappeared over the hill, the atomic mutant pushed aside the roadside bushes and lumbered back out onto the blacktop. His wolfish ears perked up as he listened to the roar of the car's motor grow fainter with distance, his heart a little heavier than it had been a few moments before.

The monster thought he'd found some new friends, but then this fat one comes along and takes them away from him. He could have intervened –

challenged this plump interloper, but something inside the beast wouldn't allow it. He knew instinctively that the fat boy was a friend to the little yellow-haired ones. He had been very gentle with them when he put them in his car. The gesture had been obvious.

The monster was sure the little ones would be safe, now, but this alone wasn't enough to comfort the brute. He felt a sadness gnawing in his cavernous chest, a loneliness that wouldn't go away. He thought briefly of going to visit the old man. Sometimes that helped to ease his sadness.

But, after a moment, he decided against it. It was late. Much had happened this day, and the creature, though he never truly grew tired, was weary of thinking and pondering. He would return to his cave and sleep. At least asleep he wouldn't be lonely.

As the drone of the car engine finally faded out altogether and was replaced by the incessant chirp of the crickets, the monster turned and lumbered sullenly off of the blacktop, through the bushes, and back into the hilly canyon beyond.

Chapter – 2

When Professor Alfred P. Willoughby opened the front door to his renovated farmhouse, Skip began to have second thoughts about bringing his two injured friends to the old man for treatment. Skip had heard in town that the old gentleman was a crackpot, and, in person, he certainly looked the part. He dressed as if he were living in Victorian England rather than twentieth century California, and his white hair, what remained of it, ringed his otherwise bald head, wild and unkempt. But, as no other medical men were available in the nearby area, Skip was left with little choice but to trust the odd looking old man.

The professor had been a bit cranky when Skip first knocked at his door, but once the boy had explained the reason for his late intrusion, the old man's manner altered at once to crisp concern. He ordered Skip to bring the injured Carlsons to a spare bedroom upstairs, where he immediately set about tending to their wounds. He moved with efficient competence, and had both assessed and bandaged the two kids' injuries in a matter of a few minutes.

Skip watched while the professor worked – his chubby, freckled face a mask of worry. "I'm sorry to bother you so late, Professor," he said after a while. "But, Doc Lawson's out of town and the hospital in San Bolero is twenty miles away."

The professor nodded casually while he wound tape around Betty Jo's sprained right wrist. "It's quite all right, young man," he assured Skip. "You did the right thing by bringing them to me. Their injuries are relatively minor – cuts, bruises and so on – but they could easily have been much more severe."

Skip's brow furrowed. "Why are they still unconscious?"

"Shock most probably," the professor replied. "A wreck like the one you described can be very traumatic, especially with victims so young." He glanced back at Skip as he finished bandaging the cut on Betty Jo's forehead. "Did you call the fire department? A fire in a bleak area like this can spread like mad."

Skip nodded. "I just got off the phone with them," he confessed. "I called Sheriff Stone, too. He and one of his deputies are on their way out to the gully right now."

At the mention of the sheriff's name, the professor turned abruptly and eyed Skip with suspicion. "Do you really think it was necessary to involve the local constable?" he demanded. "That seems like overkill to me."

Skip shrugged. "The sheriff has to know about it," he observed. "All car wrecks have to be reported."

The old man nodded. The answer appeared to placate him, but he still seemed edgy. "Yes, I suppose you're right. Routine procedure and all that."

"Sure," Skip replied.

Professor Willoughby turned his attention back to his patients. Betty Jo and Johnny, their wounds freshly tended, lay side by side on a big bed in the old man's guest room, both still unconscious.

The professor put the remainder of his first-aid supplies back in their container and then glanced back at Skip. "Well, they'll both be all right, I'd say," he ventured, "A few minor cuts and abrasions, and a nasty goose egg on each of their heads, but no signs of concussion. Both managed to sprain the same wrist, too. Uncanny." He shook his head. "I'll fetch some cool water and we'll attempt to revive them."

But, just as Professor Willoughby was about to stand up, Betty Jo's blue eyes fluttered open and she sprang up like a shot. "*Monster!*" she shrieked wildly.

"Good heavens!" yelped the professor as he fell back in his chair beside the bed, startled.

Beside him, Skip stood gaping.

Even Johnny, on the bed next to his sister, moaned and rolled into a sitting position.

Betty Jo sat on the bed, eyes wide with fright, glancing around the strange room in bewilderment. "Where am I?" she demanded.

Professor Willoughby swiftly took hold of the teen girl's bandaged wrist and patted her small hand gently. "There, there, my dear," he said soothingly. "You're quite safe, now."

"Who are you?" Betty Jo shot back, not at all soothed.

"I am Professor Alfred Willoughby," the old man said, still patting Betty Jo's injured hand. "This is my house near Brush Canyon. You and the young lad there were in rather a bad auto smash-up." He glanced back at Skip, who hovered nearby, his plump, freckly face blanched and slack. "Your young friend there found you both by the edge of the road, unconscious. Since my house was so near, he brought you to me for treatment."

The old man's answers seemed to placate the teenager and she gradually calmed down. Betty Jo noticed Johnny sitting on the bed next to her. She reached over and pulled the child into her arms. She held him against her and kissed his bandaged forehead lovingly. "The poor baby," she murmured as she settled Johnny in her lap. She glanced at the professor. "Will he be all right?"

"You both will be," Professor Willoughby promised. "Your injuries are relatively minor considering the severity of the wreck young Walters here described to me."

Betty Jo seemed to notice Skip for the first time. She smiled up at her plump neighbor. "Oh, thank you, Skip," she said gratefully. She regarded the professor. "Thank you both!"

Skip blushed and rubbed the back of his thick neck awkwardly. "You're welcome," was all he could think to say.

"Welcome, indeed," the professor added.

Betty Jo sobered a little as her aching head cleared. "May I call my father now, sir?" she asked politely.

"Of course," replied the professor. "The telephone is downstairs."

Skip stepped forward and held up a hand. "Don't bother, Jo," he said. "Your pop's not home. I tried phoning him right after I called the fire department."

Betty Jo rubbed the sore lump on her head. "Fire department?"

"Yeah. Your Chevy is a wash-out, I'm afraid. They're hauling it out of the gully right now."

Betty Jo closed her eyes and ran a hand over her bandaged forehead. Her temples were throbbing. "That's right," she said after a moment. "Daddy's at a conference meeting in Sacramento. He won't be home until sometime late tomorrow."

Johnny was beginning to squirm in her lap. "Let me up, Jo!" the child pleaded.

Betty Jo released her little brother and allowed him to crawl out of her lap and perch next to her on the big bed. "I suppose I'll have to report the accident," the girl posited.

"I already phoned it in to the sheriff," Skip explained. "He knows you and Johnny are all banged up. He said any Q&A can wait until tomorrow."

"Thank goodness for that," Betty Jo said gratefully. "I'm definitely not up to a grilling from Sheriff Stone tonight. I..." Betty Jo trailed off and her blue eyes went suddenly wide. "Wait! I must speak to Sheriff Stone! Right away!" She straightened up swiftly.

"What for?" Skip asked.

The professor looked nervous. "Now, my dear," he said as he took hold of the girl's hand once more. "I'm sure there's nothing you have to say to the sheriff that won't wait till tomorrow. You and the young lad here have endured a frightful ordeal tonight. What you both need right now is rest, and plenty of it. The report can wait."

"But, it *can't* wait!" Betty Jo insisted, pulling her hand away. "It wasn't just a car wreck. Johnny and I saw a monster out on Brush Canyon Road tonight! It's what caused me to swerve in the first place!"

Professor Willoughby went white. "A *monster?*"

"Yes," Betty Jo said with conviction, "a monster! A horrible creature of some kind, like out of a nightmare! Huge! It was standing right in the middle of the road."

Behind the professor, Skip was becoming curious. He remembered seeing something large dart across the road just as he drove up to the gully, but he decided that he had only imagined it. What if he hadn't imagined it? He gulped with fright.

Professor Willoughby looked very pale, but he maintained his composure. He cleared his throat. "Young lady, you and your brother were just in a bad automobile accident. A shock like that can do queer things to your mind. I've lived in this canyon for two months, now, and I've never seen anything wilder than a jack rabbit."

Betty Jo was growing impatient. She was tired and sore and not in the mood for condescending remarks, not even from someone as obviously distinguished as the old professor. "Sir, please don't assume I'm hysterical simply because I'm a woman," she said slowly. "I wasn't hallucinating. I saw this thing just as plainly as I'm seeing you right now."

"Yeah," piped up Johnny, "I saw him, too!"

Betty Jo looked fearful as she recalled the sight. "It was a giant of a thing," she proclaimed. "It looked a bit like a gorilla, except that it had scales, or warts, or something, covering its body instead of hair. It also looked to be wearing something – a gray, coverall type of thing, all torn-up and tattered. It might've been a radiation suit, but I'm not sure."

"I'll bet it was a space suit," Johnny chimed in. "He was probably a Martian, or something!"

"Johnny, please," Betty Jo admonished. She regarded the old man. "I don't know what it was," she confessed, "but I do know it's dangerous, Professor. It caused me to wreck my car, and who knows what else a thing like that will do if it's allowed to run around loose. Now, we must report it to Sheriff Stone right away."

Professor Willoughby's plump, rubbery face darkened and his bald pate turned a bright pink. He was clearly upset and struggling to remain calm and composed. He turned and glanced back at Skip, his bushy, gray eyebrows drawn together. "How about you, Mr. Walters," he demanded. "Did you also see this so-called beast?"

Skip looked uncomfortable. He rubbed the back of his neck and peeked over at Betty Jo. "Well, not exactly," he finally managed.

Betty Jo eyed Skip suspiciously. "What does that mean?" she demanded.

Skip shrugged. "It means I don't know," he admitted. "I thought I saw something cross the road as I drove up, but I didn't see it clearly. It might've been anything."

Johnny looked disgusted. "Boy, you're a big help!"

"Mind your manners, Johnny," Betty Jo scolded. She turned and addressed the professor, her tone level and serious. "Sir, I'd like to use your telephone."

The color again drained from the old man's face. "Please, Miss Carlson, let's not be hasty," he pleaded. "If you report a thing like this tonight to that clod of a sheriff, he'll only assume that you're still in shock from your accident. Let it go until you and the young lad have both had a good night's sleep."

Betty Jo cut her eyes. She turned to Skip. "Skip, please drive Johnny and I home. I must use the telephone." She slid off of the bed and stood.

Professor Willoughby stood up as well and took hold of Betty Jo's shoulders when she staggered. "There, you see?" he scolded. "You're still groggy from that bash on the head you took. You need rest, not more trouble!"

"Professor," Betty Jo said once her head had cleared, "I have to report what I saw. If I don't, someone's liable to be killed by that awful creature. Why, it might be outside this house right now for all we know!"

"I assure you it isn't," the professor said, but swiftly caught himself. "I mean to say that we're all perfectly safe here."

Betty Jo's pretty brow furrowed and she eyed the old man suspiciously. "Professor, are you sure you don't know something about this already?"

"I don't know what you mean," the professor evaded.

"Don't be cagey, Professor," Betty Jo chided. "You *do* know something about this, don't you?"

Johnny slid to the edge of the bed, excited. "Gee-whiz, Professor, did you make that monster in your laboratory?"

The professor was livid. *"Certainly not!"* he proclaimed staunchly.

Betty Jo raised an eyebrow. "But, you do know something about it. You've seen it, haven't you?"

"Young lady, you're being impertinent!" the old man grumbled.

"Professor," Betty Jo pleaded, "if you do know something about this, you must report it to Sheriff Stone. It's your civic duty. It could be a matter of life or death! That creature is terribly dangerous!"

Professor Willoughby sighed heavily. "I can see you don't plan to let go of this anytime soon," he observed with glum reticence. "You are a very stubborn young woman."

Skip suppressed a chuckle. "You have no idea," he declared.

Betty Jo folded her arms impatiently. "This is no time to be glib, Skip," she pointed out. "This is a very serious situation."

Professor Willoughby nodded. "Perhaps you're right, my dear," he relented. "The secret couldn't have lasted for long, I suppose."

Betty Jo frowned. "Secret?"

"Yes, secret," the professor replied crisply. He looked the three kids over and shook his head, uncertain. "It seems I'll have to put my trust in the three of you," he posited. "I certainly hope that trust won't be misplaced."

Betty Jo looked confused. "Professor, you're speaking in riddles."

"It is a bit of a riddle, the whole nasty business," the old man observed. "But, it seems I'll have to reveal it to you before you unintentionally commit a tragic blunder."

"What are you talking about, sir?"

The professor stepped aside and gestured. "If you three will join me downstairs in the parlor, I'll try to clear things up for you. I only hope that when I do, you'll try to be more understanding."

Betty Jo, Skip and Johnny all exchanged glances, and then filed out of the guest bedroom with the professor close behind them.

In her mind, Betty Jo was beginning to have misgivings. She hoped that she hadn't bitten off more than she could chew by getting mixed up in this business. But, even if she had, it was too late to back out now. By insisting on knowing about the creature, Betty Jo had committed herself, along with Skip and little Johnny. Sometimes, the girl mused, it might be wiser just to keep one's mouth shut.

Chapter – 3

Betty Jo was impressed as they came downstairs and entered the parlor. She recalled that, only a few months before, this farmhouse had been little more than an abandoned ruin. But, in a remarkably short period of time, the puttering old scientist had worked wonders with the place.

The parlor had been paneled in oak, and a new marble mantle piece put over the old fireplace. New wallpaper had been put up, and fine paintings – some portraits, some landscapes – were hanging on every wall. There was a magnificent, old grandfather's clock ticking away in a corner near the mantle, and a charming array of ornate vases perched atop every end table. Brand new leather furniture adorned the room as well; a deep burgundy in color, and a glorious, Oriental rug was laid out in front of the fireplace.

"Oh, Professor, you've done a wonderful job renovating this old farmhouse," Betty Jo trilled. "Your taste is exquisite!"

"Oh, bosh," said the professor, waving a pudgy hand dismissively. "I couldn't pick out a set of drapes without an instruction manual. I hired a decorator and workmen to do all this."

Skip looked around at all the expensive furnishings and gave a low whistle. "You must be rich," he observed.

"I am," the professor declared nonchalantly. He gestured. "Won't you please sit down?" When his three guests had seated themselves on the sofa, the professor regarded them. "Now, before we begin, is anyone hungry? I must confess that I, for one, am famished."

Johnny rubbed his empty belly. "I'm sure hungry," he admitted.

"I could eat a horse!" Skip put in.

Always conscious of her diet, Betty Jo was a bit less obvious about her enthusiasm. "Perhaps something light," she said diplomatically. "It is rather late."

"Fine," said the professor. "You three make yourselves comfortable. Meantime, I'll round up something to eat. I do hope you like soda pop. I fear I've developed rather a weakness for the stuff since I've lived in your country."

"I love soda pop!" Johnny blurted out.

"Good," said the professor. "I shan't be long." That said, the old man turned and hurried out of the room.

When he was sure the professor was out of earshot, Skip faced the two Carlson siblings. "Maybe I should've risked taking you two to the hospital in San Bolero," he postulated. "Unless I miss my guess, that old coot is a few bats shy of a belfry."

"Oh, nonsense, Skip," Betty Jo scolded. "He may be a little eccentric, and I do think he's hiding something from us, but he's not crazy."

"I think he's swell," Johnny proclaimed. He beamed up at his sister. "Gee, sis, do suppose he has a laboratory right here in his house?"

"Oh Johnny, honestly," Betty Jo scoffed. "You read too many comic books! I doubt he has a laboratory at all. He's probably retired. He must be past sixty."

Johnny waved a hand. "That doesn't matter," he insisted. "Mad scientists don't retire. I'll bet he's got a hum-dinger of a laboratory down in the basement!" Johnny's blue eyes lit up. "Why, he's probably got an atomic reactor down there, and maybe a robot, and probably a gorilla locked up in a big, old cage!"

Betty Jo looked exasperated. "You and that wild imagination of yours," she chided. "I think we won't be seeing so many of those silly science fiction pictures. They're obviously giving you bad ideas!"

"Aw, phooey!" Johnny complained.

Skip looked thoughtful. "Just what is it you think he's hiding from us, Jo?"

Betty Jo shrugged. "Only he can tell us that," she replied. "My guess would be that he's seen that thing in the canyon before, but doesn't want anyone to know about it."

"But, what for?" Skip inquired.

"Probably he wants to study it," Betty Jo theorized. "He is a scientist, after all. Only this time, he's picked a subject to study that's liable to bite his head off!" She glanced at Skip. "It's lucky for him we found out about this before it was too late."

Skip was worried. "Just how far do you think that old goat will go to keep his nutty secret?" He was suddenly alarmed. "You don't suppose he'd try to..."

Betty Jo cut him off, "Poison us?" She laughed. "No, Skip. I'm sure he's perfectly safe." Just then, a wave of pain shot through Betty Jo's head and she put up a hand to steady herself.

"What's the matter, Jo-Jo?" Johnny asked, concerned.

"It's just my head," Betty Jo replied. "That bump I took, it throbs something awful if I move wrong."

Johnny rubbed his own sore bump and winced. "Mine, too!"

Skip shook his head. "You two had both ought to be in bed," he pointed out. "You were pretty well banged up in that wreck. Plus, it's past ten o'clock."

Betty Jo rubbed her weary eyes. "I'd sure like to be in bed," she confessed. "But we can't leave here until we've heard the professor out and settled this business."

Skip shrugged. "You're the boss."

At that moment, the professor returned wheeling a cart containing a hastily prepared meal of lunchmeat sandwiches and bottles of cherry cola. "Dinner is served," he announced. "Only simple fair, I'm afraid. But anything heavier at so late an hour might ward off sleep, and we'll all need plenty of that."

There were no arguments from the three kids. Everyone collected their sandwiches and cola and dug in. No one spoke as they all ate. In spite of his age, the professor was done first and waited patiently for his three guests to finish before addressing them.

"Well," the old man began as the three kids finished up, "I trust our bellies are all full, now, and that we may proceed with the business at hand?"

Betty Jo dabbed her full lips with her napkin daintily. "We're finished, Professor."

"Fine," the professor remarked. He took a deep breath and regarded his three guests solemnly. "Now, are you three quite sure you want to be let in on this thing?"

Betty Jo spoke for them. "Very sure," she proclaimed.

The old man's eyes narrowed. "Very well," he said grimly. "You may be sorry afterwards, I warn you..."

"We'll take that chance, Professor," Betty Jo asserted.

"All right," the professor continued, "but before I spill a single word of it to you, I must first have your promise that you won't repeat it to anyone. Is that clear?"

"We can't make you a promise like that," Betty Jo protested. "Our whole purpose is to warn people about that horrid creature so that it can be destroyed before it harms or kills someone."

The professor shook his head bitterly. "No, no! You don't understand! You must listen to me! When I've finished, then you can judge for yourselves. But, I won't tell you a blasted thing if you're going to be so bloody arbitrary!"

"There's no need to swear at us, Professor!" Betty Jo admonished. "How can we possibly judge anything for ourselves if you won't tell us anything, and how can we promise to keep quiet about something if we don't know what it's all about?"

The professor took off his rectangular spectacles and rubbed his tired eyes. "I'm only asking you to have open minds," he said at length. "Not to rush to a judgment until you have all the pertinent facts."

"We get that, Prof," said Skip.

"Yes," Betty Jo added. "But, we won't have those facts until you divulge them."

"True," the old man relented. He sighed and pulled a face. "If I don't tell you, you'll run to that nincompoop of a sheriff, and if I do tell you, you probably will, anyway." He looked glum and desolate. Finally he shrugged. "Rather a narrow window of choice you've left me"

Betty Jo tried to console him. "We promise not to do anything until you've given us all the facts."

The professor's face tightened. "Well, I suppose that's the best I'm going to get from you lot," he barked.

"I'm sorry, it is," replied Betty Jo flatly.

The professor ran a pudgy hand over the ring of tangled, white hair that ran around the back of his mostly bald head. "I further suppose that should I refuse to comply with your empirical little demands that I will be implicated in all this, if not directly, then indirectly for failure to cooperate?"

Betty Jo folded her arms impatiently, but didn't reply. The gesture alone, however, was plain enough.

"I see," said the professor bitterly. It was clear to him that the headstrong teenager intended to have her own way, or else. "Very well," the old man relented. "But, I warn you, it's a long story, and not a very happy one. By the time I've finished, you may find yourselves questioning your own government."

"We're waiting, Professor."

"Some stories are best left untold," the old man lamented after a moment of silent reflection. "Man is a fragile beast, fearful of the dark and of unknown things. And when he lifts the veil and peers into the primordial darkness beyond, he sometimes finds… *monsters.*"

The professor paused long enough to take a sip from his bottle of cherry cola, and then continued.

"Science is a wonderful instrument. It opens doors for man, and solves riddles long pondered by the philosophers. But, in the wrong hands, well… it's a bit like a loaded gun in the hands of a small child. It becomes an instrument of destruction rather than one of knowledge. And when fear and suspicion become the taskmasters of man, he becomes a beast again, and the world around him a jungle."

The Unthinkable Hybrid

The professor leaned forward in his leather armchair and regarded the three young people sitting on the sofa across from him. He let his dark, serious eyes drift over each innocent, round face. Inwardly, he marveled at the sweet ignorance behind those faces, the as yet untarnished and carefully cultured purity. Spoiling such purity seemed shameful and left the old man feeling guilty. Still, they had insisted he let them in on this terrible secret. Like Prometheus of old, they had demanded knowledge, and as he did, might come to suffer for having it.

Professor Willoughby was thoughtful as he reached for his bent briar pipe and the tartan pouch of tobacco that rested on the end table beside his chair. He slowly stuffed the pipe with the tobacco as he continued.

"I often wonder what would have befallen the human race had Adam not reached for that bloody apple. Would we really be any worse off? I don't know." He found himself chuckling softly, reflectively. "Funny sounding talk coming from a scientist I admit, but, perhaps, appropriate all the same. It does a man good to reflect – to wonder whether or not the path he's chosen to follow is the correct one."

The professor struck a match on his rough, tweed trousers, lit his pipe, and then puffed on it slowly as he postulated.

"I suppose it all began with the coming of the *Atomic Age*. When mankind let that genie out of its bottle, there was no putting it back. Now, we're caught in a deadly trap of our own making and forced to live along the edge of fearful precipice where our penchant for self destruction might finally accomplish exactly that."

The old man's face darkened. "For the first in man's blood-stained history it may be possible to accomplish what floods, volcanoes, ice-ages and a myriad of other natural and unnatural disasters have failed to do – wipe out the human race." The professor looked glum. "And, sadly, it was science herself that gave man the means to do this."

"The atomic bomb," said Betty Jo thoughtfully.

"Yes," the old man confirmed. "And the hydrogen bomb, and all the others that are sure to follow in the wake of the first two." The professor's voice betrayed the weariness that hampered him. "Bloody *fools*!" he spat bitterly. "But, I'm to blame, too. I had a hand in the horrid business myself, so who am I to pass judgment."

Skip looked at the old man, a little awed. "You worked on the atom bomb?"

The professor nodded. "Yes, for the War Department. I was at Oak Ridge, and Los Alamos. I was at White Sands when they exploded the first one, may God forgive me." He looked doubtful. "Assuming there is a God."

"There *is*," Betty Jo said decisively.

The old man looked at the girl. His was a world-weary soul, and Betty Jo's bright, youthful confidence was bolstering. "Perhaps," he conceded. "But, he is a neglectful Deity to allow his Children to wander so far from the path."

"Men wander off on their own," Betty Jo pointed out wisely. "It's up to us to shepherd ourselves."

The professor nodded. "Well spoke," he admitted. "And we do a bloody bad job of it most of the time." He leaned back in his armchair and puffed quietly on his pipe for a moment. "I am guiltier than most men, however. I lent my knowledge to those travesties, so I must answer for any evil that results from them."

His dark eyes wandered slightly. "Oh, I consoled myself – told myself it was for the greater good. There were the Nazis to best, and the Nipponese Warlords. I assured myself that the bomb was the only viable solution." He shifted uncomfortably in his chair.

"But that doesn't wash the blood entirely off my hands. The stains of it are still there. Hiroshima, Nagasaki – a hundred thousand men, women and innocent children obliterated in a nuclear holocaust." The professor's face was grim.

"Some of my colleagues and I saw the evil of it before the others and pulled out. But, there were plenty of other eager fools ready to fill our boots. And plenty of war-mongering generals equally eager to exploit them."

"Hey, it was a war, Prof," Skip pointed out. "You did what you had to do. Don't beat yourself up over it."

"Hmmph!" scoffed the professor. He stood suddenly, clasped his hands behind his back and began to pace the parlor, his plump, rubbery face dark and sullen. "Oh, that's a fine enough excuse," he barked. "But tell that to the survivors of Hiroshima, or to the crew of the *Lucky Dragon*, or to all those poor islanders who suffered radiation burns after that last H-bomb test in the Pacific. Those excuses sound a bit hollow, then."

He ceased his pacing and returned to his chair, seating himself slowly. "No. Man must accept responsibility for his actions – try to atone for his sins, if you will."

Betty Jo watched as the old man puffed silently on his pipe for a moment. She felt sorry for him. Clearly, he was tormented by his involvement in the nuclear nightmare that now engulfed the world, but he was also wandering off the track. The teenager decided it was time she corralled him.

"Professor," she consoled, "I'm as sorry for all those people as you are. But, you aren't to blame. The military men made those decisions, not you scientists. Besides, what has all this to do with that creature?"

"Everything," replied Professor Willoughby. "That creature, as you call him, is the product of misused science – a *Frankenstein* of the Atomic Age."

"Golly!" gulped Johnny.

The professor dumped the ashes from his pipe into an ashtray, and then re-filled the bowl from his tartan tobacco pouch. "I had gone back to chairing the *Theoretical Science Department* at Owens University in Berkley after the war. I was determined not to have anything more to do with government business. But, that business went on fine without me, driven, as always, by fear and suspicion. However, now that the Japanese and the Nazis were beaten, a new foe had to be created to fuel that suspicion – the Soviet Union."

"The Commies," gasped Skip.

The old man nodded. "Yes, the Commies – dreadful new boogie men, sure to make off with your wives and children if you let your guard down for a moment. And worse, these boogie men are armed to the teeth with atomic weapons." The professor lit his pipe and eyed Skip coolly. "You think precisely as your leaders do – with dread and suspicion behind your words."

"Aren't the Commies enough to scare you?" Skip demanded.

The professor shook his head. "Not the communists themselves," he confessed. "But, it's the fear that drives them to the same madness as your own leaders. That I'm very much concerned about."

His face grew darker still. "That fear is almost a palpable thing, both here and in Russia. It's a hideous, mind-bending thing that claws at men's brains and makes them loathe their neighbors and distrust their brothers. Fear is the chief architect of this nuclear nightmare that's got the world in a stranglehold, and it's also what fathered *Project Omega*."

Betty Jo's brow furrowed. "Project Omega?"

Professor Willoughby nodded. "That's what they called it. A fitting name, I must say."

"What was Project Omega?" Skip asked.

"An outgrowth of the nuclear program," the professor revealed, "and of another program called *Operation Paperclip.*"

"Operation Paperclip?"

"Yes," confirmed the professor. "Your government began recruiting many of Nazi Germany's best minds right after the war and placing them in charge of certain areas of national defense, such as the nuclear program and the new rocket program. Many of the men recruited had been ardent Nazi party members during the war, and hadn't changed their stripes. One man in particular, a fiend by the name of Heinrich von Kepler, held the reins at Project Omega."

Skip looked incredulous. "Are you telling us that the government has *Nazis* working in the Defense Department?"

Betty Jo swallowed. "I don't believe that."

"I don't either!" Johnny growled.

The professor took a sip of cola. "Never the less, it happens to be true. The Soviets are doing the same thing. Each side is determined to get the upper hand in this preposterous Cold War, and both are willing to go to any lengths to do it."

"That's a *lie!*" Skip barked. "The Russians would do that, but not us!"

"Wait, Skip," Betty Jo said quietly. She regarded the professor. "Go on, sir," she urged. "You were about to tell us about Project Omega."

"Project Omega was Von Kepler's brainchild," the professor explained. "He convinced the Joint Chiefs to sign off on it, and to fully fund it. He used their fear of a nuclear confrontation with the Soviets to hedge his bet. It worked like a charm." The professor shook his head bitterly. "Frightened men are easier to dupe than rational men. That's how the world got into this dreadful state."

"But, what *was* Project Omega?" Betty Jo demanded.

The professor stood up once more and began to pace the parlor, his hands clasped behind him. "According to the proposal that Von Kepler handed in to the State Department, the goal of Project Omega was to develop a serum that would adapt human cells to the after effects of an atomic bombardment. He insisted he had devised a theory by which a chemical solution could be used to stave off the damaging effects of extreme radiation and allow human cells to conform to the new parameters introduced by the gamma rays."

"Not only would the affected cells not die, they would continue to grow, using the energy provided by the radiation itself as fuel. Of course, the cells would have to change drastically in order to contain that energy, and that meant mutation."

Betty Jo and Skip exchanged a glance.

"But," the professor continued, "Von Kepler claimed he could control the degree of mutation so that it wouldn't be overly harmful. In this way, people treated with his chemical solution wouldn't die during an atomic war. They would survive to rebuild the world."

"But, what's wrong with that?" Skip challenged. "It sounds like the answer to all our troubles."

Professor Willoughby shook his head ruefully. "Only if you happen to be one of the selected few to receive the serum," he revealed. "You see, only the military leadership, top government and business leaders, certain wealthy types, and a small number of craftsmen, tradesmen and laborers were to benefit from Project Omega. The serum was never intended to be shared with the common folk."

"I see," said Betty Jo. "Well, I suppose it'd have to be that way. There'd be so little food and water left after such a war. You'd have to save only the best and brightest people…" she trailed off sadly.

"*Best* is a very generic term," the professor countered. "How does one estimate a word like that? I'd say a humanitarian outranks a general, or some corporate bigwig."

"But, that's not what the fathers of Project Omega were thinking. No. They were only thinking of saving their own rotten necks, and Von Kepler sold them a scenario that played out exactly as the leaders wanted it to."

"However, it was a lie, right from the start. Von Kepler had plans of his own, and they didn't mesh with the ones laid out in the Project Omega Proposal."

"What plans?" Skip demanded.

"Diabolical ones, I assure you," replied the professor. He puffed on his pipe as he roamed the parlor, stopping occasionally to regard one of his paintings. "I'm sure all of you know one of Hitler's mad dreams was to build up a so-called *master race* – a race of blonde supermen that would dominate the future. Unless I miss my guess, Von Kepler had similar plans in mind at Project Omega, but his scheme backfired on him."

"Backfired how?" Betty Jo asked.

The professor held up a pudgy hand. "Before I get into that, I'd better make the rest of it clear."

He strode back to his chair and eased into the seat. "Project Omega went into operation in 1953. Von Kepler and a selected group of hand-picked assistants were provided with a special facility in the Nevada desert a few miles from the California border."

"In the beginning, they stuck fairly close to the outlined goals of the project – trying to produce a serum that would arrest the damaging effects of radiation on living tissue. Of course, at first, they experimented only on lab rats and monkeys."

"In the early going, there were many failures, as would be expected. Many of the lab animals died, either from radiation poisoning, or from the chemical agents themselves – some of which turned out to be highly toxic."

"Von Kepler's specialty was genetic engineering and, I must confess, he was a brilliant researcher – years ahead of anyone else in that area of study. He eventually found a solution to the problem. It took him about two years to do it, however, and the Brass at the Pentagon was becoming impatient with the apparent lack of progress at the facility."

"The Pentagon threatened to cut the funding to Project Omega unless Von Kepler could offer up proof of definite progress within a given time frame. He, for better or worse, succeeded."

The professor leaned back in his chair as he recalled. "He produced a young rat that, after being exposed to over a thousand curies of radium, not only didn't die, it continued to grow and get stronger. The officials were convinced that Von Kepler was on the right track and let the project survive."

"Von Kepler went on to produce three more rats and one monkey that, after being injected with his X-14 formula, were able to survive massive doses of radiation without dying, or growing ill. The project seemed a success."

"But, success with mere lab animals didn't satisfy Von Kepler. He wanted a *human* test subject. He pushed for volunteers among his staff and among the unfortunate Marines assigned to guard the facility. But, to Von Kepler's disgust, he had no takers."

The professor's face saddened as he continued. "Then, late one night in the summer of 1955, fate intervened on Von Kepler's behalf. A family, the Morgan family, was driving through the desert on their way from Nevada to California. Carl Morgan had been offered a job in California, and rather than drive every day from Nevada, he opted to relocate. He took his wife, Beryl, and their teenage son, Christopher, along – a fateful decision, unfortunately."

Betty Jo was beginning to feel uneasy. A premonition was creeping into her mind, but she preferred to hold it at bay. "What happened?" she asked, uncertain that she really wanted to know the answer.

"Nearly the same thing that happened to you tonight, Miss Carlson," the professor replied. "There was a rockslide on the canyon road along which the Morgans were driving. To avoid the slide, Carl Morgan turned sharply, *too* sharply. Like you, he went off the road, through the guardrail, and plunged into a steep ravine."

"The boy, Christopher, was somehow thrown out of the car during its descent into the gully, but he struck his head on a rock and was left comatose."

The professor paused to re-light his pipe. "The car rolled on, slammed into a boulder at the base of the gully, and burst into flames. Carl and Beryl Morgan had, evidently, been knocked unconscious. Sadly, they were both consumed by the fire."

Betty Jo reached for Johnny's small hand and squeezed it. "That nearly happened to us," she remarked with a shudder.

Johnny pushed close to his sister. "It sure did!"

Professor Willoughby leveled a meaningful gaze on the two Carlsons. "I know," he said cryptically. "You two were very fortunate. I think for a reason, but we'll get into that later on."

The old man puffed steadily on his pipe for a moment, then continued. "As I said, Christopher Morgan had been thrown clear of the car before it hit the boulder, and so was spared from the flames. But, he'd struck his head in the bargain and was left in a coma there in the burning gully."

"By sheer happenstance, an elderly farmer and his wife were driving along that lonely desert road that night and spotted the fire. They chose to stop and investigate. They found young Morgan, barely alive, and carried him to safety."

"There were no hospitals in that remote region, so the old couple took the boy to what they believed was a military base a few kilometers away. But, it wasn't a military base at all. It was the Project Omega test facility."

Once again, Betty Jo was left with a feeling of ominous dread. It clung to the outer reaches of her senses, and she continued to resist it.

"Ordinarily," the professor continued, "the Marine guards at the gate would have turned the old couple away, but regulations stated that they had to call in for instructions under such circumstances. The guards were surprised when Von Kepler ordered them to bring the boy inside."

"Von Kepler thoroughly questioned the old farmer and his wife about the accident, and learned of the death of the boy's parents. And, after the old couple had gone, he ordered a squad of Marines to clean up the accident site and dispose of the remains."

A strange, cold light came into the professor's eyes as he went on with his story. "At last, Von Kepler had what he'd wanted all along – a human test subject, a comatose pawn on which to try out his formula."

Finally, the feeling of dread that had been clawing at the fringes of Betty Jo's mind burst into her brain as full-blown horror – a final realization of her fears that left her trembling from head to foot.

"Professor," she gasped, "are you saying that dreadful creature we saw tonight, that *monster,* was once a *human being?*"

Beside her, Skip and Johnny jumped slightly – both completely blindsided by Betty Jo's revelation.

"That's exactly what I'm saying," the professor confirmed grimly. "He was a boy no older than you are, Miss Carlson – a destitute boy with no family to miss him and no friends to mourn him. It was a perfect storm of injustice… perfect for Von Kepler, that is."

For a time the three kids sat in stunned silence, each of them struggling to grasp the monstrous implications of what the strange old man had told them. The story seemed impossible. Such a travesty might have occurred in Nazi Germany, or in the Soviet Union, but surely not in America.

The professor puffed on his pipe and watched the troubled expressions on the faces of his three young guests thoughtfully. He allowed them a little time to process the horrendous information he had just given them.

Again, he felt somewhat guilty. It seemed a shame to burst their bubble of security with such lurid details and spoil their carefully nurtured pseudo-reality. To these children, America was the bastion of serenity and purity, a golden place where horrors were forbidden and ugliness carefully soiled over.

But, they had asked for the truth, and this was the truth, pure and unvarnished. Even the prettiest rose has thorns, the shiniest armor has blemishes, and, as sure as night follows day, there is a dark side to every paradise.

"I...I can't believe it," Betty Jo muttered quietly.

"I *don't* believe it!" Skip declared angrily. "I wasn't sure before, but now I am! This old goat is *crazy*, just like everyone in town says! He doesn't know what he's talking about! Things like that don't happen in America, or anywhere! He's got a screw loose, I'm telling you!" Skip ran a hand through his thick, greased-up hair, stood up and stalked around the sofa in a huff, his heart racing.

The professor kept his voice level when he spoke again. "Denying the facts, or my sanity, won't make what I've told you any less true, Mr. Walters."

"It *isn't* true," Skip shot back from behind the sofa. "It's a crazy cock-and-bull story, that's all!"

"Skip, please sit down," Betty Jo pleaded. "It has to be true. Remember that Johnny and I saw the thing."

"You saw *something*," Skip retorted. "You don't know what it was. It might've been anything! Hollywood is only about forty miles from here, you know. It could've been some creep in a costume – a publicity stunt for some cheese-ball science fiction picture. That makes a lot more sense than anything this old coot has said tonight."

"Skip, please," Betty Jo begged.

The professor remained cool throughout this interchange. He sat, quietly puffing on his pipe, his face grim and unreadable. At last, he spoke, "If the crazy old coot may be permitted to continue…"

"Please do," Betty Jo prompted.

"Believe me, Mr. Walters," the professor declared, "nothing would please me more than to have all this turn out to be a delirious old man's pipe dream. But, alas, it isn't. It is all, unfortunately, only too real."

The professor laced his thick fingers together and waited as Skip returned reluctantly to the sofa. When the plump teenager had seated himself again, the old man went on.

"As I've already explained, young Morgan was in a coma when he was brought to Project Omega. As far as I know, he never came out of that coma – not as a human being at any rate."

"Over the next eight months, Von Kepler experimented on the boy's helpless body, trying out various versions of the formula. Once Von Kepler had refined the concoction enough to reduce the harmful effects of the gamma rays, he began phase two of the procedure – *nuclear infusions*."

"He exposed Christopher to a myriad of isotopes: Cobalt-60, Strontium-90, U235 – the whole range of deadly elements. Eventually, he exposed young Morgan to more radiation than was set loose with the explosion of *Trinity* – enough to kill thousands."

"But, the boy didn't die. Instead, his cell structure began to radically alter, to *mutate*. It didn't happen overnight. It took months. But, eventually, he transformed into the thing you saw tonight out on the canyon road – a mutant *Hercules* with the strength of thousands and a body all but indestructible. He had become the world's first *Atomic Man*."

"Golly," Johnny breathed quietly, "an Atomic Man!"

"An Unthinkable Hybrid to be more precise," the professor declared. "A walking junk-heap composed not only of the features of both mammal and reptile, but also of the organic and the inorganic."

"His outer hide is metallic, like pig-iron, which explains his tremendous weight and durability. Somehow, the mutation process magnified the quantity and type of metallic elements already present in his body."

"It also awakened in him animal genes long dormant in his human cells, which accounts for his monstrous appearance."

"That's awful," Betty Jo observed. "And *stupid*! Why would that horrible man want to do something like that? I thought the goal of the project was to help human beings survive an atomic war? If they cease to be human in the process, then the whole thing is pointless!"

"Of course," the professor agreed. "I'm afraid we may never learn the true goal of Project Omega. If it was an attempt to create a superhuman master-race, then it was a failure as well."

"I don't think Von Kepler planned for the mutation to go as far as it ultimately did. He didn't intend for the end product to be so inhuman – so animal. But, the process he started got out of his control and went beyond the parameters he had in mind."

Skip, his arms folded once more, at last had to speak. "Assuming all this isn't just a lot of hot-air, how did *you* become privy to this hush-hush, top secret stuff?"

"Although I had left government research long before then," the professor replied patiently, "I was still well respected by many in the State Department. After rumors of what Von Kepler might actually be doing at Project Omega finally made their way back to Washington, the decision was made to pull the plug on the project before word leaked out to the public, or worse, to the Russians."

The old man rubbed his pudgy hands together briskly. "That, Mr. Walters, is where I enter the story."

The professor stood up suddenly and began to prowl the parlor once more. "I was approached by the officials to join a special team of civilian and military inspectors who were sent to first investigate, and then put an end to Project Omega."

"I accepted only reluctantly at first, but, once I learned who was in back of Project Omega, I became adamant. I had always despised Von Kepler, even before he joined Hitler and the Nazis. It would be a pleasure to dress down that scoundrel, whatever the circumstances."

The professor turned and regarded his guests with renewed vigor, his hands clasped tight behind him.

"We arrived at Project Omega in early March of this year, and despite protests from Von Kepler that he was not yet ready to release his results to us, we proceeded with the investigation."

"Although he was furious, Von Kepler had little choice but to give us a tour of the facility, and reveal to us the notes and data he'd accumulated during the course of his research."

"While this material satisfied most of the others in our party, I demanded to see the end result of the experiment."

"With a great deal of reluctance, Von Kepler took us to one of the smaller labs in the compound and showed us the rats and monkey he had described in his progress reports."

"The creatures were all alive and apparently healthy, but each bore characteristics not described in the reports. They had all lost their hair and grown a crude, leathery covering, dotted with metallic warts – characteristics similar to the beast you two saw on the canyon road."

"Von Kepler assured us that this condition was a fluke – a side effect of extreme radiation saturation that he hoped to correct in future experiments. Obviously, he never did correct it."

"In spite of everything he'd showed to us, I still wasn't satisfied. The reports had mentioned a mysterious, new test subject, a so-called *Subject-X*, which was only briefly and vaguely described. Even at the time, I had a foreboding suspicion regarding this Subject-X, but I wanted confirmation."

The professor resumed pacing. "Von Kepler adamantly refused to reveal anything in regard to Subject-X, insisting that it was still in the experimental stage, and that the information was classified at the highest level."

"Fortunately, Mr. Fitzgerald of the State Department was along with us, and he had clearance at the highest level of your government. Fitzgerald ordered Von Kepler to produce Subject-X for our inspection."

"Von Kepler knew the Marine guards at the facility would obey Fitzgerald's orders over his own, and this forced him to comply."

"He took us, finally, to Project Omega's main laboratory, which was a fairly impressive affair, complete with its own atomic reactor and nuclear storage facility."

"There, strapped to a huge, metal slab, still, at the time, in a coma, was the mutant goliath that had once been Christopher Morgan."

"He possessed the same gruesome physical aberrations as the rats and monkey we'd just seen – a leathery, blackish hide covered in silvery, metallic warts."

"Despite his monstrous appearance, it was clear to me straight away that this loathsome behemoth had started out a human being. The basic shape and upright posture were dead give-aways."

"Even some of the others realized what they were looking at and were filled with dread and disgust. Only that war-mongering General Considine was impressed. Fortunately, he was out-voted."

Finally, the professor seated himself and began to re-fill the bowl of his pipe with tobacco.

"Fitzgerald had Von Kepler arrested on the spot and confined to quarters. After contacting the State Department and informing them of the situation, he gave the order for the immediate shut-down and dismantling of Project Omega."

"Everything was to be destroyed – the notes, the reports, the equipment, even the facility buildings. The government wanted nothing to remain of Project Omega."

"The facility guards were all sworn to secrecy, as was the inspection team. The leaders wanted nothing left that the press or the public might learn about. Nor did they want any rumors to sprout up that the Soviets could latch onto and use as political leverage."

The professor looked grim. "Of course, this meant that the test subjects – all of them – were to be destroyed as well." He shook his head sadly. "I was charged with this task due to my advanced scientific knowledge."

"I had no desire to undertake the task, nor was I certain it was even possible. These creatures had been created to survive in a deadly, post-nuclear world. Their bodies had been forged into iron-hard enigmas capable of withstanding tremendous force."

"Not only that, one of the subjects was a human being. After reading Von Kepler's hidden, secret dossier on the brute, I learned his identity, and of the deadly accident that had killed his family and left him comatose."

"I had Von Kepler's Nazi thoroughness to thank for this. He had, apparently, dug deeply into the boy's past in order to more easily erase it and thus cover up his crime. That same thoroughness served to convict Von Kepler, thanks to his penchant for carefully documenting his every move."

Professor Willoughby paused long enough to light his pipe and then continued.

"Now that I knew exactly who it was lying strapped to that slab in the main laboratory, my mission was made all the more difficult."

"Your government was quite clear in their instructions, even after I made it known to them that

Subject-X had once been a young man. The order stood."

Professor Willoughby looked bitter. "It was reasoned by the higher-ups that the poor brute was no longer human, and so destroying him would not classify as murder."

"Plus, he was in a coma, which amounted to little more than death already. No matter what arguments I gave them, they insisted that Subject-X had to be destroyed along with the rest of Project Omega."

Betty Jo and Johnny exchanged a sad glance. The girl reached for her kid brother and pulled him closer to her. She stroked his blonde hair gently.

The professor forged on. "With a heavy heart, I decided to comply with the orders. I rationalized that if he were to come to and find himself in such a horrid state, he might well wish for death."

"Granting him that boon while he still lay in a coma, safely shielded from his hideous fate, might be kinder in the long run than fighting to save him."

"There was still, however, the problem of *how* to destroy him. Since his body was very nearly invulnerable, shooting him was no good. I'd have to find another way."

"I decided that a chemical approach was the soundest, surest way. He was, after all, born of chemicals and isotopes. Perhaps, then, it was fitting that he should end by them as well."

The professor leaned back in his chair and puffed on his pipe.

"I decided to test my theory first on the corrupted lab animals – the three rats and the monkey. Like young Morgan, their condition had been brought about by exposure to extreme radiation and the resulting mutations were similar."

"Apparently the physical attributes – the metallic hide, the immense strength – were natural adaptations to nuclear saturation. It appeared to be a conditioned genetic response, in all four cases, to a massive influx of high-energy gamma rays, initiated, no doubt, by Von Kepler's chemical formula."

"Keeping all that in mind, I decided to approach the matter in a different way. I would not treat the affected animals as organic life forms, but rather as the nuclear-powered automatons that they, in fact, were."

The old man leaned forward.

"I decided to introduce a cadmium compound into their systems via a gas I developed right there in the lab. The gas was impregnated with microscopic particles of cadmium that, when inhaled or ingested, would serve the same purpose in these mutants as cadmium control rods do in an atomic reactor – to dilute the nuclear response."

"The experiment was a success. When I exposed the rats and monkey to the cadmium gas, the nuclear reaction in their bodies gradually came to a halt, rendering them dormant – dead, for all intents and purposes."

The professor leaned back in his seat once more. "And, having succeeded with the lab animals, I knew I could do the same for poor Morgan."

"Clearly, you didn't," Betty Jo pointed out.

"Obviously, no," replied the old man. He stood up and, again, began to prowl the parlor, puffing away on his bent briar as he spoke.

"I had discussed my intentions with my scientific colleagues at the facility, and we were all agreed on my approach. We knew that if the cadmium gas rendered the animals dormant, it would also work on the boy, and we were fully prepared to make the attempt."

"However, fate – fickle lady that she is – decided to intervene. On the very night we were planning to attend to Subject-X, the beast suddenly woke from his coma, burst his bonds, smashed his way out of the test facility, and escaped into the desert."

"Wow!" exclaimed Johnny, impressed.

The professor hung his head. "We had failed," he admitted sadly. "The Marine guards pursued the creature, but he managed to elude them in a sand storm out on the wasteland."

He shrugged. "Even if they'd caught up to him, they'd only have been killed trying to capture him. Bullets, as I've told you already, can do him no harm."

The professor returned to his chair and sat down again. "The creature's escape was not the worst of it, however..."

"It gets worse?" Skip griped.

"I'm afraid it does," confessed the old man. "It had been decided by the officials that Von Kepler would be held at the test facility, under house arrest, while the shut-down was going on so that he could supply answers when they were needed – a bloody stupid blunder, in my opinion. He should have been sent to a maximum security prison straight away. But, alas, such was not the case."

"During all the commotion caused by the creature's escape, Von Kepler, probably with the aid of a confederate, disappeared as well. So far as I know, he's still at large."

There was a gasp of alarm from all three kids.

"You mean that Nazi madman is on the loose right now?" Betty Jo gulped.

"I'm afraid he is," Professor Willoughby confirmed. "And he is probably seeking the creature himself. Not only that, I suspect he was backed by a group of secret conspirators from the beginning; possibly a remnant of the German-American Bund Movement. This group may be hiding him and probably helping him to locate the monster."

"Jeepers!" yelped Johnny.

"Indeed," agreed the professor.

Skip raised a skeptical eyebrow. "Speaking of which, just how did *you* locate the monster?" he demanded. "I thought you said that test facility was in Nevada? How'd he wind up in California?"

"The facility was near the California border," the professor clarified. "When the beast escaped, it prowled the desert for a month before it migrated to this area."

"I appropriated some equipment and transportation from Project Omega and pursued the creature almost at once. You see, I knew something about him those military clods didn't."

"What was that?" Betty Jo asked.

"That he was radioactive, of course," the professor proclaimed. "That's why Von Kepler put the radiation suit on him – to retard the gamma rays he gave off."

"But, how did that help you to find him?"

"Elementary, my dear," explained the professor. "I had only to scan the desert with a Geiger counter to pick up his trail. I followed him for weeks. I finally found the poor brute hiding in the old rock quarry pit in Brush Canyon."

"When I'd located him, I bought this house and a sizable chunk of the canyon territory so that I could be nearby and, hopefully, find a way to help him."

"So, he's living in *Ghost Rock Cave*," Betty Jo remarked thoughtfully. She looked up. "That's what the kids in town call the old quarry pit. It opens into a real cave further inside. I used to go exploring in there when we first moved to Maplewood."

"I know about the cave," said the professor. "I explored it as well. It's the ideal place for young Morgan to hide until other arrangements can be made."

"What other arrangements?" Skip demanded. "I thought you were under government orders to kill the thing. You mean you're not going to follow those orders?"

The professor stood up again. "May I remind you, Mr. Walters, that I am not a citizen of your country, and therefore not under any obligation to follow the orders of your government."

Skip folded his arms angrily. "If you're living here, then you have to follow our laws," he grumbled. "And if you're not a citizen, then why have you been here so long?"

"I was invited here prior to the war by your government to aid in certain scientific research," the professor answered quietly. "It was a special arrangement that simply extended due, in large part, to the war."

"The war's been over for eleven years," Skip pointed out. "What's keeping you?"

The professor turned pink. "You are an impertinent young whelp!" he barked. "And you have the manners of a barnyard swine!"

Johnny laughed. "He sort of looks like one, too!"

Skip raised a pudgy fist at Johnny, but Betty Jo intervened.

"Boys, please," she pleaded. She faced the professor. "Sir, do you think you really can help him? Christopher Morgan, I mean."

The old man sighed. "I don't know," he admitted. "If you mean can I change him back into a human being, then no. The mutation has gone much too far for that. I might be able to arrest any further changes in his cells, but, scientifically speaking, that's the best we can hope for."

He leaned back in his chair. "But, I can keep him out of the hands of the military. That would, at least, save his life."

Betty Jo bit her lip and looked thoughtful. Then, her blue eyes lit up. "Oh my Gosh, I just realized," she burst out. "It was *him*! *He* did it!"

Johnny looked up at his sister. "What do you mean, Jo-Jo?"

"It was him," Betty Jo insisted again. "Christopher Morgan. He was the one who pulled us out of the wreck!" Her eyes darted rapidly as she remembered. "I recall going through the guardrail and down into the gully, but not coming back up. He must have come down, rescued us, and carried us back up the bank!"

"Yeah!" Johnny piped up. "He must have! He sure is a swell guy for a monster!"

"That's *crazy*!" Skip objected. "How would a thing like that have brains enough to rescue anybody?"

Betty Jo looked at the professor. "He could have, couldn't he, sir?"

The old man grinned and nodded. "Of course he could have."

Betty Jo smiled warmly. "You knew from the beginning, didn't you, Professor?"

The professor nodded once more. "I suspected, yes," he confessed. "Your accident must have stirred memories in his brain – memories of what happened to his parents. He couldn't allow you and little Johnny to share the same fate."

Betty Jo smiled again and pulled Johnny into her arms, holding him close. "Then he's still human inside," she beamed. "Oh, that's wonderful!"

"Perhaps not human exactly," the professor observed wisely, "but, at least, more humane than most men."

Skip, however, was not convinced. "Oh, this is just dandy," he complained. "Now, he has you two corrupted!" He regarded Betty Jo grimly. "You know what he's going to do now, don't you? He's gonna ask us to keep quiet about all this, even though it's our duty to turn him and that whatever-it-is over to the army. You can see that coming, can't you, Jo?"

"Aw, go soak your head, fat-chicken!" Johnny barked.

Betty Jo cupped her soft palm over her little brother's mouth. "Hush, sweetheart," she commanded. She faced Skip calmly. "Now Skip, let's not be too hasty about this..."

Skip gaped incredulously. "Too *hasty*?" he snapped. "An hour ago you were aching to run to the sheriff and calling for the thing's head!"

"That was before I had the facts," Betty Jo pointed out. "Now I do have the facts, and I've

changed my mind." She smiled persuasively. "I think
you ought to change your mind as well."

Skip gawked at the beautiful blonde. "*Do* you?"
he chirped sarcastically. "Well, I *haven't!* In fact, I'm
surer than ever, now, that we should turn this old coot
in and be done with the whole business! He's already
admitted to committing treason! If we get dragged into
this, who know what will happen to us?"

"How can I be a traitor to a country I don't
belong to?" the professor demanded.

"If you don't belong here, then *leave!*" Skip
shot back angrily. "And take your pet monster and that
Gestapo guy along with you!"

"Von Kepler was a scientist, not a Gestapo
man," the professor corrected.

"That's beside the point!" Skip grumbled. "This
is none of our business! We're just high school kids.
How can we possibly help you in the first place?"

Betty Jo glanced irritably at Skip. "All the
professor is asking us to do, Skip, is not to broadcast
what he's told us tonight." She looked at the old man
for confirmation. "Yes?"

The professor spread his hands and nodded.
"That's all I ask."

Skip stood suddenly and began prowling the
parlor. "That's *enough* to ask!" he growled. "You

know perfectly well, Jo, that if this old goat can find that thing, the military is bound to find him, too. When they do, they might start asking questions – try to find out who knew about it. Then it won't only be his neck in the noose, it'll be *ours!*"

"What young Walters says is quite true, Miss Carlson," the professor admitted. "The military will never stop looking for that poor brute until they've found and destroyed him."

The old man smiled weakly. "Plus, I've made rather a bad name with them myself, I fear. I will quite understand if you want nothing to do with either of us."

"Nonsense!" Betty Jo said decisively. "Christopher Morgan saved our lives tonight – Johnny's and mine. He did this in spite of all the horrible things that have happened to him. We'll be forever grateful to him." She smiled down at Johnny, who was still perched in her lap. "His secret is safe with us."

"It sure is!" Johnny chirped.

The professor laced his stubby fingers together and looked up at Skip. "That leaves only you, Mr. Walters," he observed. "Are you going to allow a misguided view of patriotism trump your basic human decency?"

Betty Jo and Johnny looked hopefully up at Skip over the back of the sofa.

Skip turned away from their eyes and leaned against the grandfather's clock, his troubled mind in a muddle. His father was a World War II veteran and ardent patriot who had taught Skip from a young age to respect the flag and the laws it symbolized.

As far as Skip was concerned, the government and military were representatives of the orderly democracy he'd been taught to revere and were, therefore, almost sacred institutions. If they believed that something ought to be done away with for the good of the country, then who was he, or these others, to question that decision?

On top of that, if the Russians or the Chinese ever got wind of what went on at Project Omega, it'd be a propaganda boon for them, and a blow to America.

On the other hand, Skip did love Betty Jo Carlson and had great respect for her opinion. He knew her to be a kind and just girl who let her heart guide her in such matters. Skip was torn between his loyalties.

"Well, Skip," Betty Jo prodded gently. "Have you decided?"

At last, Skip sighed. He still kept his eyes turned away from the others. The meek tone in Betty Jo's voice neatly drowned out the refrains of his father warning him against those who were soft on patriotic duty. It was a hard decision for Skip, but, at length, he made it. Finally, he turned and faced his fellow conspirators.

"All right," he relented. "Maybe we'll get lucky and no one will find out about it." He shrugged. "Anyway, what've I got to lose? They can only arrest me, right?"

The professor smiled. "That's the spirit, my lad," he encouraged. "You're made of stouter stuff than I first supposed."

"Oh, thanks," Skip snorted, unsure whether the comment had been meant as a compliment or an insult.

Slowly, he made his way back to the sofa and seated himself beside Betty Jo and Johnny. To Skip's delight, they were both smiling gratefully at him.

The professor stood up and faced the three kids with renewed vitality. The ruddy complexion natural to the old man had returned to his cheeks. "Not to worry, my young friends," he declared cheerfully. "Although fraught with a certain degree of peril, I'm certain this little pact of ours will not go unrewarded."

"I hope you're right about that, Prof," Skip said sullenly. He felt Betty Jo's small, soft hand on top of his own and he smiled weakly at her. Ordinarily, a gesture like that from his beautiful neighbor would have sent Skip into orbit. As it was, it only offered him mild comfort.

The plump boy sighed inwardly. All the conflict that had boiled up in him only moments before lingered inside him, like a mass of hot coals, slowly smoldering. Now, too, was added a familiar, but equally unwelcome element – fear. A half a dozen frightful scenarios began to run through his mind, and none of them played out well for him. At last, he swallowed hard. "What have I gotten myself into?"

Chapter – 4

Sheriff Samuel T. Stone stood on the edge of the canyon road and watched as the few members of the Maplewood Fire Department milled around in the gully below, making sure there were no embers left from the fire to be blown away by the cool, night breeze.

The fire had been out for some time by now, but, in dry regions like this, it was better to be safe than sorry.

Stone was a fat, thick-fisted man in his mid fifties with heavy jowls, a crew cut, a permanently pink face, and a brow worn in what seemed like a perpetual scowl. In his tan colored sheriff's uniform and cowboy-style hat, Stone looked rather like an obese John Wayne, and acted the part most of the time.

He was strictly a law-and-order man and had little patience for what he considered 'Tom Foolery'. The local teenagers were the bane of Sheriff Stone's existence, and whenever there was something amiss in Corman County, those under the age of twenty were the first suspects in his mind.

He stood observing as the blackened remains of Betty Jo Carlson's burned Chevrolet Bel Air was hauled out of the gully by Clete Scroggins' tow truck, shaking his bulldog of a head reproachfully.

"Damn shame," he muttered. "Give some teenage brat a fine new car like that, and they go and pile it up in the gully."

He turned to his deputy, a thin, less than confident looking young man named Scott Brady. "Did you get a hold of Carlson?" he demanded.

"No, sir," admitted Deputy Brady. "I tried, but Dr. Carlson wasn't at home."

"Figures," lamented the sheriff. He shook his head. "I never liked that guy. Those college professors are all a bunch of flakes. It's no wonder their kids turn out the way they do." He went on shaking his head, his mouth scrunched in a thin line.

Deputy Brady glanced at Stone. "Betty Jo and Johnny are pretty good kids," he remarked. "I see 'em both at church most every Sunday."

The sheriff waved a ham-sized hand dismissively. "That don't mean nothing," he grumbled. "You're just soft on that girl 'cause you're sweet on her."

Deputy Brady blushed and remained silent.

"If she were such a good girl," the sheriff demanded, "would we be out here at ten thirty at night puttin' out a fire and haulin' her burned-up car out of the gully?"

"Just an accident, sir," Deputy Brady replied.

"Accident my *foot*!" Stone barked. "She was probably out here, whippin' around in that Bel Air, goin' over the speed limit, and lost control. Dern women drivers! No female oughta be behind the wheel of an automobile! 'Specially no *teenage* female!"

Deputy Brady kept quiet. He knew better than to argue with his superior when he was in a cantankerous mood – which was most of the time.

Clete Scroggins, the heavy-set, scruffy garage mechanic, crawled out of the cab of his beat-up tow truck and sauntered over to the two lawmen. "She's all set to tow, what's left of her, Sam," he told the sheriff. "You need anything else?"

Stone shook his head. "Nah, Clete. Haul it outta here. We'll work out the details Monday mornin'."

Scroggins eyed Stone suspiciously. "What about the tow fee?" he asked. "You want me to bill the county?"

"Hell no I don't!" Stone thundered. "That bill is goin' straight to that pantywaist college professor, Doc Carlson. Why should the taxpayers pay for his brat's carelessness?"

"Just as long as the bill gets paid," Scroggins pressed.

"It'll get paid," Stone barked. "Carlson may be a sissy, but he ain't lackin' for money. Now, get goin', Clete. I want this business cleared up in the next thirty minutes. I'm dead on my feet!"

Scroggins climbed back in the cab of his tow truck, started the motor and trundled away toward town with the ruined car.

At the same time, Captain Ross Miller of the Maplewood Fire Department trudged up out of the gully, brushing ashes from his coveralls, and stood beside Stone and Brady.

"How's it look, Ross?" the sheriff asked.

"It's out," replied Captain Miller. "Fortunately, that gully is pretty arid – not a lot of stuff down there to burn. The tree and all the dried grass and weeds went up quick. We'll have to drive around for an hour or so to be sure that none of the embers have drifted, but I'd say it's whipped. There isn't a lot of wind tonight anyway."

"Glad to hear it," said Stone. "The last thing we need around here is a wildfire gettin' started. 'Specially with the citrus groves bein' so close."

The fire chief nodded. "You can say that again."

"Well, if you boys think you've got it, I don't reckon there's any need for Brady n' me to hang around. We may as well head back to the ranch."

"Yeah, go ahead, Sam," said Miller. "You look like you're fixing to drop, anyway."

Stone chuckled. "I am feelin' a might baggy," he admitted. "I'll stop by the fire house Monday and fill out the reports."

"Fine," said the fire chief. "I'll see you Monday, then." He waved goodbye, then trudged back into the gully to consult with his crew.

Sheriff Stone turned to his deputy. "Well, c'mon, Brady," he said, gesturing toward the prowl car. "Let's get back to the station."

But, as the two men were about to cross the road, they noticed a dark green Buick sedan coming down the canyon road toward them. The car slowed as it neared the two lawmen and finally stopped alongside them.

Sheriff Stone and Deputy Brady exchanged a curious glance.

The back passenger's side window rolled slowly down, and the lawmen could see a dark figure looking out at them. They stepped closer.

"You want somethin', mister?" asked the sheriff as he leaned near the door and peered in at the shadowy occupant.

The man in the backseat of the Buick leaned out, giving the sheriff and his young deputy a better look at him. They both recoiled slightly at the sight of him.

The man was a strange sight, indeed. He was a tall, thin character with a bony, hairless face and a sharp, hawk nose. He had a long chin with a prominent cleft in it and a thin, slit of a mouth that, when he smiled, bore tall, yellowed teeth. He wore a dark green trench coat with a matching, broad-brimmed felt fedora and, perhaps queerest of all, his eyes were hidden behind a sinister-looking pair of dark goggles.

After staring a moment, Sheriff Stone leaned closer. "Somethin' on your mind, buster?"

"Please excuse me," the fearful looking man in the backseat said in a thick, German accent. "My two associates and I are looking for the residence of an old colleague of mine. I had heard from my sources that he now resides in this canyon somewhere. We had hoped you might help us to locate him." The lean figure grinned menacingly.

Stone and Brady exchanged glances, and then peeked in the window at the two hulking figures occupying the front seat. Although hard to make out in the gloom, one man was taller than the other, and both wore dark topcoats and fedoras.

"What's the name of this colleague of yours?" Stone finally asked.

"Professor Alfred Willoughby," the goggled man said. "He is an Englishman in his early sixties, white hair, fattish, dresses in old-fashioned clothing, very domineering. Do you know him?"

The sheriff nodded. "I've seen him around," he admitted. "You must mean the old Limey coot who bought that broken-down farmhouse out in Brush Canyon."

The goggled figure grinned. "Yes, that is who I mean," he said. "Can you direct us to where this broken-down place, as you call it, is located, Sheriff?"

The fat lawman raised a meaty arm and pointed. "Just keep on the canyon road for about a mile," he replied. "There's a big mailbox on a post by a bend in the road. It marks the driveway. You can't miss it."

The grim figure smiled again. "Thank you, Sheriff. You have been most helpful."

"Uh-huh," grunted the sheriff. "Say, what's with the dark goggles at night, Fritz? You got a problem with folks gettin' a good look at your face?"

The goggled man merely grinned once more. "I'm afraid my eyes were once very badly damaged," he professed. "Since the injury, they have become hypersensitive to light. I am forced to wear these goggles at all times."

Sheriff Stone was suspicious, but too tired to press the matter. He gestured to the two burly figures in the front seat. "Who are these goons? Come to think of it, who are you?"

"I am Dr. Kraus," the hairless man lied. "And those two gentlemen are my laboratory assistants. We've come to compare notes with Professor Willoughby regarding an experiment we've been conducting."

The sheriff raised an eyebrow. "A bit late to be visitin', ain't it?"

The goggled man shrugged. "Science has no time table, Sheriff," he proclaimed. "Professor Willoughby's input is crucial to the success of our experiment."

Stone eyed the man. "You don't say?" he said flatly. "Does the old gent know you're comin'?"

The goggled man laced his bony, gloved fingers together, and the grin finally faded from his cadaverous face.

"Nein," he said coldly. "I'm sure our visit will come as a complete surprise to him."

"Whatever you say, Fritz," the sheriff remarked. "We won't keep you."

The goggled man merely nodded and rolled up the window. A moment later, the big, green Buick was slowly, silently trundling away.

Sheriff Stone and Deputy Brady watched, puzzled, until the car disappeared around a bend in the road.

When it was out of sight, the deputy turned to the sheriff. "What do you make of that guy, Sheriff?"

"Sounded like a Kraut to me," the sheriff declared.

"How about those two gorillas in the front seat?"

Stone shrugged. "I didn't get a good look at 'em," he admitted. "But, they didn't look like egg-heads to me. More like Ruskies!" He shook his head in disgust. "We got all kinds of foreigners over here since the war ended. Damn shame."

"You think we ought to tail 'em?" the deputy asked. "They may be up to no good!"

Stone shook his head. "Let them foreigners tend to their own business," he declared. "All I wanna do right now is go home and hit the hay." He turned and lumbered toward the squad car.

Deputy Brady, however, lingered for a moment. He felt terribly ill-at-ease about the three menacing figures that had driven off in the green sedan. They sure looked like trouble to him.

"Get a move on, Brady!" Sheriff Stone called from the patrol car.

Brady tarried a moment longer, then turned and trotted back to the squad car, hoping that the warning bell ringing in the back of his mind was merely a false alarm.

Chapter – 5

The grandfather's clock in Professor Willoughby's parlor struck eleven, and the bells sounded out in the big room. Betty Jo yawned wearily and noticed that Johnny, who was cuddled up on the sofa beside her, was very nearly asleep himself.

"My goodness," she observed. "It's getting quite late. I'd best get Johnny home and put him to bed."

"Aw, I'm not sleepy, sis" Johnny objected, but he nuzzled under her chin and shut his eyes all the same.

Betty Jo scooped the child up and nestled him against her. "Oh, you're sleepy all right, space captain." She kissed his forehead. "It's way past your bedtime, and mine, too." She glanced over at Skip. "Would you mind driving us home, Skip?"

"Of course I will," Skip replied. He stood.

"You're all welcome to spend the night here," the professor offered. "Heaven knows I have plenty of room."

"No, thank you, Professor," Betty Jo said as she stood up with Johnny in her arms. "I'm sure we'll all sleep better in our own comfy beds."

"As you wish," said the professor. He stood up as well. "But, at least, let me walk you to your car."

"Do you want me to carry Johnny, Betty Jo?" Skip asked.

Betty Jo shook her head. "I've got him," she replied. "I'm the only one he'll let carry him." She regarded the professor. "Thank you, sir, for your hospitality, and for treating our injuries. I hope we can repay you somehow."

The old man smiled. "The promise you gave me is payment enough," he told her. "That and your friendship."

Betty Jo smiled warmly. "You have both," she assured him. "For keeps."

"That's fine," said the professor. "Secrets are hard enough things to keep, and are a burden on one man alone. Shared they are more bearable, I think."

"Ah," came a familiar voice from just outside the doorway, "but secrets are fleeting things, and often very dangerous to keep. Is that not so, Herr Professor?"

The professor and the three kids were all startled by the voice with the thick, German accent, and whirled in their seats to face the doorway. There, blocking the only way out of the room, stood three, large, fearful looking men in dark overcoats and broad-brimmed fedoras.

The two on the end were thick-bodied and powerful; one taller and lantern-jawed, the other shorter and bulldog-faced. But, it was the tall, lean man in the middle who was, by far, the most disturbing. Peering out from under the wide brimmed hat was a face only slightly more than skeletal, hook-nosed and entirely devoid of hair. His skin had a sickly, yellowed pallor, his mouth was merely a slit, and his eyes were hidden behind an ominous pair of dark goggles. It had been this man, with his German accent, who had spoken.

Betty Jo gasped in fright and pulled Johnny close to her. Johnny, for once unashamed to show his fear, clung to his sister.

Skip gulped and stepped behind the professor's chair, anxious to put space between him and these frightful intruders.

"Guten abend, Herr Willoughby," the lean man in the goggles said, a nasty grin forming on his thin face. "I trust you remember me, Englander?"

The professor's pink face went white, but his voice boomed as he barked out the goggled man's name. *"Von Kepler!"*

Across from the old man, Betty Jo squeaked with fright and exchanged a terrified glance with Skip. She felt Johnny burrow under her chin and cling tight to her neck.

Skip stood behind the professor's armchair shivering, his knees knocking. Courage was not among his chief virtues at the best of times, and right now it had deserted him completely.

"Yes, Von Kepler," the lean man said smoothly as he glided panther-like into the parlor with his two burly henchmen trailing close at his heels.

"Permit me to introduce my two associates." He indicated the taller, square-jawed man, "These are Comrades Miroff," then the shorter, bulldog-faced man, "and Petrovitch. It seems that the Soviet Union is also interested in the product of my genius."

"C-Commies!" gulped Skip.

Betty Jo was white-faced and speechless.

Professor Willoughby was not the timid sort, and although he was well aware of the danger he and his young guests were facing, he tried to put up a brave front for them.

"Get out of my house, you Nazi scoundrel!" he snapped angrily. "And take those two communist hoodlums with you! Unless you'd like me to call the sheriff!"

Von Kepler merely chuckled. "Don't be an imbecile, Willoughby," he laughed. "Any more than you can help. It was that fat fool of a sheriff who gave us directions to your doorstep. Besides, we took the liberty of cutting your telephone line when we came in."

"Oh..." Betty Jo shuddered. She felt faint, but did her best to keep from passing out. She had never been so frightened.

Beside her, Skip was shaking noticeably. If possible, he was even more afraid than Betty Jo.

In his sister's arms, Johnny, too, was quaking with fright. He clung tight to Betty Jo, hoping with all his might that Professor Willoughby would think of a way out of this terrible dilemma.

For his part, the professor was fresh out of ideas. He knew they were in a very bad spot. All he could think to do was stall for time. "What do you want, Von Kepler?" he demanded.

"You know perfectly well what I've come for," the Nazi said darkly. "The Project Omega test subject. He is, after all, my creation."

"You're mad if you think I'll give him to you," said the professor.

Von Kepler glanced subtly back at his two companions and, almost at once, the two Russians drew automatic pistols from their overcoats and trained them on the professor and the three kids.

Betty Jo gasped and clung tight to Johnny.

Von Kepler smiled wickedly. "And you're mad, my dear Willoughby, if you think we will be leaving this rustic place without him."

The German moved closer. "So you may as well dispense with the foolish heroics and tell me where he is hiding."

"Shooting us will do you no good, Heinrich," the professor proclaimed boldly. "We can tell you nothing if we're dead."

"There won't be a need to shoot all of you," Von Kepler observed slyly. "One would be sufficient to loosen the tongues of the others."

"Leave these children out of this, Heinrich," the professor pleaded. "Your quarrel is with me! Besides, they know nothing. They merely came to me for first-aid."

Von Kepler looked over the three kids thoughtfully. "I see," he said as he stepped closer to

Betty Jo and Johnny. "Then, it was their vehicle being towed out of the gully as we passed."

"It was," confirmed the professor. "Now, let them go. They were preparing to leave anyhow, when you and those two ruffians came barging in here."

Von Kepler regarded Betty Jo and smiled, bearing ugly, yellowed teeth. "You are quite lovely, my dear."

"Thank you," Betty Jo said frostily. She was filled with disgust, but shivering at the same time.

"I do hope you and the little one were not too badly harmed in that unfortunate accident?" Von Kepler prodded.

"We're fine," Betty Jo replied, taking a step back.

Von Kepler merely stepped forward. "You are a local girl, I presume?"

"I am," said Betty Jo nervously. "We're all locals."

Von Kepler nodded. "I see. Then you know the area well?"

"Of course," Betty Jo answered. "Why?"

The German shrugged. "Mere curiosity."

Professor Willoughby came forward, gripped Betty Jo's shoulders, and pulled her and Johnny, whom she still held tight in her arms, away from the curious Nazi.

"Nothing can be gained from accosting these children, Heinrich," the old man insisted. "Let them be on their way, I tell you. Then you and I can have it out between us. Alone."

Von Kepler smiled. "Still playing the *noble hero* I see, Alfred," he observed blandly. "You British always think you can handle anything."

The shorter of the two Russians, Petrovich, finally spoke up. "Why do we waste time?" he demanded in a thick Russian accent. "If he will not talk, there are ways we can *make* him talk!"

Betty Jo gasped again and pressed into the professor's arms.

Behind them, Skip was quaking like a leaf in the wind. His teeth were chattering and his hands trembling and all the color had drained from his plump, freckly face. His mind had seized up on him so that all he could do was watch the unfolding events in a fear-fogged daze – a fright coma that paralyzed him from head to foot.

Von Kepler raised a gloved hand. "Have patience, comrade," he said calmly. "You Russians are too eager to employ force. Subtlety is often a far more effective tool."

He turned around and ran a finger over a vase that perched on the mantle above the fireplace. "You will be reasonable, Alfred, if we permit the children to go?" He again faced the professor.

"You have my word, Heinrich," said the old man.

Von Kepler nodded. "I know you to be a truthful man," he admitted. "I accept your word."

Petrovich brandished his automatic threateningly. "You cannot do that!" he barked. "They know too much! They may talk!"

"Oh, but we won't!" Betty Jo stammered quickly. "We promise!" She turned to Skip behind her. "Right, Skip?"

Too terrified to speak, the fat teenager merely nodded stupidly.

Von Kepler strode slowly around the room and paused near the three kids. He observed them for a moment through his dark, sinister goggles. "That is true," he said quietly. "They may talk..."

Professor Willoughby faced the German without fear. "You either let the children go, Heinrich, or we have no deal! Take it or leave it!"

Von Kepler smiled coldly. "I grow weary of your childish bravado, old man," he declared with venom in his voice. "It is becoming quite tiresome.

I'm afraid we will have to resort to less civilized methods."

Von Kepler gestured and Petrovich lumbered forward like a sauntering gorilla.

The Nazi then turned his attention to Johnny, who was still clutched in his sister's arms. He reached for the child. "Come here, my fine lad…"

Betty Jo screamed and tried to move away, but the burly Petrovich seized her shoulders and held her in a cruel, unbreakable grip.

She clasped Johnny tightly to her, but Von Kepler easily pried her slender arms away and grabbed the struggling seven-year-old. Johnny was yanked brutally from his horrified sister's grasp, and Betty Jo was held fast in the brawny Russian's vice-tight grip.

Johnny was terrified, but shrieked and kicked and fought back with all his meager might. The German, however, swiftly subdued the child and held him pinned with a lean, but powerful arm.

Betty Jo went wild, heaving and struggling like a caged lioness and shrieking for all she was worth. But, for all her fuss, she couldn't budge the grip the big Russian had on her.

Petrovich pinned her flailing arms and pressed her small body against his thick, muscled bulk until the screaming teenager could barely move.

"Silence her," Von Kepler ordered, annoyed with Betty Jo's shrill, relentless shrieking.

Petrovich clamped a huge, gloved hand over Betty Jo's mouth, smothering the terrified girl into silence.

The professor rushed forward and grappled with Petrovich. "Take your hands off of that child, you Slavic barbarian!"

Von Kepler gestured and the hulking Miroff stepped in, seized the professor, and shoved him roughly into Skip. The tall Russian drew his gun, trained it on the two men, and herded them away from Von Kepler and Petrovich. Miroff then held Skip and the professor at bay with his pistol while his compatriots went ahead with their grim business.

With his adversaries all safely subdued, Von Kepler proceeded. He held Johnny close to him with one lean, strong arm while he fished in the pocket of his trench coat with his free hand. A moment later, he produced an object that was not at once identifiable, as it was largely concealed by the German's gloved hand. He brought the object up near Johnny's face as he regarded the professor slyly.

"You are stubborn, Englander," he said, slightly out of breath from his exertions. "But not so stubborn, I'll wager, to trifle with me any longer. Am I right?"

Professor Willoughby snorted in disgust. "You are a *beast*, Heinrich! You have even fewer scruples than I supposed! Leave these children out of this, I implore you!"

Von Kepler's grin morphed into an ugly frown, and he held up the object he'd fished from his coat pocket for all to see. It was a switchblade knife! He pressed the button on the hilt and a sharp, shining, five-inch blade flashed out with a vicious click. Von Kepler brought the glinting blade near to Johnny's terrified, tear-streaked face.

Horrified, Betty Jo renewed her hopeless struggles, tears gushing from her wide blue eyes, but it was useless. In the big Russian's grip, she was as helpless as a baby and could only stare in anguished silence at the frightful events unfolding before her.

"Hold still, girl!" Petrovich barked and squeezed the squirming teenager until she sagged limply in his brawny arms.

"My patience is at an end, old man," Von Kepler said icily as he brought the shining blade within inches of Johnny's face. "Perhaps depriving the whelp of his nose would loosen your tongue? Or an ear?"

Johnny was absolutely frozen solid with fright. He could neither move, nor cry out. He could only hang stiffly in the German's arms and stare, wide-eyed, at the vicious blade held before his face – transfixed by the sharp, glinting point.

Professor Willoughby held up trembling hands, "No, no," he pleaded, his voice quavering for the first time. "Please don't harm the lad! I'll tell you anything you want to know!"

Von Kepler smiled. "Yes," he said with a deadly calm in his voice, "I know you will." He closed the blade on the knife and gestured to Miroff.

The tall Russian put away his pistol and approached the Nazi.

Von Kepler swung Johnny around and handed him off to Miroff, then chuckled as he pocketed the switchblade. "You see, comrades? He can be reasonable when given the proper motivation."

With Johnny hanging limply in his arms, sobbing quietly, Miroff glanced disgustedly at Von Kepler. Although a seasoned KGB operative and a decorated Red Army soldier, Miroff was not a common thug. He had descended from a long line of honorable fighting men in his family.

He was loyal to his country and a good agent for the Kremlin, thanks to his military background, but he did not subscribe personally to the Cold War paranoia that dominated his government. Nor had he any desire to terrorize helpless children. There was no honor in such activities for a man like himself.

On top of that, he as yet hated the Nazis for the travesties they had committed against his countrymen during the war. Still, he was under orders from the Kremlin to cooperate with this savage, and it might prove dangerous for his family in Moscow if he failed to complete his mission.

Miroff glanced at the child in his beefy arms, then over at the blonde girl hanging in the grasp of his comrade, Petrovich. The girl was pretty with her round face and soft, golden curls. She resembled his youngest sister, Katrina, and seeing her manhandled in such a way angered Miroff, but there was little he could do about it.

He dared not protest. It might arouse suspicion in regard to his loyalty, and such things, he knew, were not tolerated by the Kremlin.

Miroff took small comfort in the fact that his orders also dictated that, once the creature Von Kepler had created was in Soviet hands, the Nazi was to be liquidated. He grinned slightly at the prospect, and hoped fervently that he would have the opportunity to do the job.

Miroff decided it was best to bide his time. He held the sobbing boy as gently as he could, and even stroked the child's head to comfort him when he was sure his two associates were not looking.

Von Kepler approached Professor Willoughby, a triumphant grin fixed on his skeletal face. "Now then, Herr Professor, with all the foolish histrionics out of the way, shall we proceed with our business?"

Professor Willoughby let out a defeated, hapless sigh and nodded grimly. "It seems I have no alternative."

"That is true," Von Kepler agreed. He gestured to the sofa. "Shall we be seated and be comfortable?"

Without protest, Willoughby and Skip seated themselves on the sofa, while Von Kepler eased himself into the professor's armchair across from them.

Betty Jo and Johnny remained prisoners in the arms of the two burly Russians.

When he was comfortable, the Nazi crossed his bony legs and laced his long, gloved fingers together. "Very well," he oozed silkily, "you may begin, Alfred. But, be warned – it will prove very unpleasant for these young people if you attempt to deceive us. Am I clear, old man?"

The professor nodded sullenly.

"Excellent!" chirped the Nazi. "Now, proceed."

Chapter – 6

The full moon gleamed above the arid, craggy hills of Brush Canyon, bathing the rock-strewn vista below in its ghostly illumination. Great clumps of weeds, groupings of yucca plants, the occasional juniper tree, or lonely, looming oak, broke up the otherwise rocky, sand-covered terrain and added a touch of color to an otherwise brown and dusty world.

Though it looked to the casual observer to be a dead world, the canyon, like the true desert regions further west, was very much alive and teeming with living things. Animals of every type and variety combed the arid hills seeking sustenance from a land less barren than one might suppose.

Coyotes prowled in search of small game, and foxes, too. Rattlesnakes and king snakes slithered over the sand, and beetles and tarantulas scuttled amid the cooling rocks. Big desert hares with strong legs and long, alert ears hopped over the moonlit land, nibbled at plants and were careful of their foes. Tortoises pulled into their shells for the night while small bats twittered in front of the moon, chasing moths and June bugs on their leathery wings.

The atomic behemoth lumbered over the hills, headed for the old, disused rock quarry pit where he'd made his home. He had been roaming among the rocks for some time, feeling lost. His mind was muddled and somberness had come over him since his encounter with the little yellow-haired humans on the road some hours before.

The fiery car wreck had stirred memories in the radioactive brute – memories of a time before the Bad Place. Memories his simple, mutant brain could only half understand. He had been left lonely and confused after the encounter and now sought solace in the hills, as he always did when troubled.

He startled a female deer and her young fawn that were coming down from the high country to have a drink at the pond not far from the old quarry pit. They fled as the mutant beast stumbled over the rocks near them, and dashed back up into the craggy bluffs above.

The monster watched them go a little sadly. Most creatures avoided him – ran whenever they saw him approach. He was too hulking and clumsy to have ever caught them, but the animals didn't seem to know that. Something about him drove the other beasts away.

Even the coyotes, cougars and wildcats seemed afraid of him. Everything feared him, a fate that weighed on the brute like a millstone hung about his neck.

He paused for a moment and looked around him. A big hare sitting a few feet away, gnawing contentedly at a sprig of green on the desert floor, bolted at the sight of the lumbering goliath.

The monster snorted unhappily. He stood for a moment lamenting his predicament in a vague, uncomprehending way, when the sound and smell of rippling water came to his ears and nostrils.

He went tromping down the bank, pushing aside bushes and interfering boulders until he came to a tree-lined glen surrounding a fairly respectable pond. Had he been able to read, a sign posted near the water named it *Simmons Pond*, but the monster cared little about such things. To him, the pond was merely the pond – a place to get water.

It was the one place the other canyon beasts didn't flee from him, unless he came too close to them as they drank. After a long, hot day wrestling with the domineering sun, all the creatures of Brush Canyon came to the pond to sate their thirst, including the atomic monster.

In the belly of the beast rested a nuclear reactor of organic make – a mutation that allowed his huge body to reconstitute energy on a continual basis with no need for external fuel. However, although eating was not essential to the radioactive brute, water was needed regularly as a cooling agent. And so, the beast came to the pond nightly to sate his immense thirst, along with the rest of his canyon neighbors.

As he entered the peaceful glen, the monster noticed several other creatures taking their nightly drink, while others still tended to different business at the water's edge. The pond proved to be a busy place, especially after dark.

A pair of feisty, well muscled raccoons was poised on a rock by the water's edge, waiting for any small fish to swim within reach of their swift little paws.

In the immense old oak that loomed over the water, a stately owl perched and watched the brushy hills around the pond for the scurry of mice. Occasionally, he announced his presence by ushering an echoing hoot from the branches above.

Across the pond, another doe and her fawn were drinking one last time before heading back to cover for the night. Near them was a husky rabbit, who sat nibbling happily at the variety of bushes that grew along the edge of the pond, and washing down each mouthful with cool, clear water.

A pair of foxes – a mother and her kit – slinked out of the bushes and dipped their slender, black-nosed muzzles in the water. Predator and prey alike came to the pond to drink, and a temporary truce developed between them as they lingered there a few moments in the moonlight. Once they returned to the lonely hills above, however, all bets were off.

Even the atomic monster seemed to go largely unnoticed as he lumbered through the bushes and paused near the water's edge. Only the rabbit that was nibbling at the bushes near the monster scurried away when the radioactive behemoth crouched by the pond and leaned out over the water.

He reached down with a massive paw to scoop up a drink when something caught the monster's eye and he paused a moment. He noticed, first, the bright, silvery image of the moon – a flat, shining disc floating there in the black water, swaying and undulating with the gentle current made by the cool, evening breeze.

The beast was puzzled at first by the image in the water, for it looked familiar, as if he'd seen it elsewhere. Finally, his dull mind remembered and he cast his cat's eyes up at the clear night sky. There, the shining, silvery, spring moon hung, unimpeded by the clouds, casting its shimmering, celestial light down on the canyon from its place in the heavens.

It was a peaceful sight – soothing, even to the tormented monster. The moon offered solace in its ghostly light, a sense of tranquility its proud brother, the sun, could never equal. This was why the mutant preferred to prowl by night. Like all night creatures, he felt a certain comfort in the embrace of darkness and the knowledge that most of his potential foes were safely dreaming.

His gaze lingered briefly on the moon above, but, inevitably, his simple brain was capable only of meager contemplation and he lost interest in the heavens and turned his attention back to the shimmering pond water.

He saw the image of the moon floating there, just as before, but, this time, another image dancing in the black water caught his attention. At first, the image was difficult to make out in the fading light, but as the beast focused his feline eyes, the image grew clearer.

It was a frightful image, indeed – a monstrous face, like an ape's and a crocodile's at the same time. The atomic goliath yelped in fright and recoiled from the image. But, as he did so, he noticed the image recoil as well. He paused, his primitive brain in a whirl. It took several moments to collect what few simple thoughts he had.

When he was over the shock, the monster took another look in the pond water and, sure enough, the horrible, gnarled face was there again, staring back at him with glaring, fiendish, catlike eyes that burned as if lit from within by some terrible energy.

The monster opened his mouth in a fright, and, likewise, so did the image floating in the pond, bearing a gaggle of horrendous irregular fangs as it did so.

Again, the mutant behemoth recoiled in terror, and, just as before, so did the horrific image in the water.

At last, the truth dawned on the poor, dim brute. He peeked back in the pond water and saw the awful face and, like with the moon above, knew it must be a reflection – a reflection of his *own* face!

He reached up with a steely talon and touched his face to be sure, and so did the figure in the water. The monster grimaced at the touch of his talon and pulled back his paw to inspect it better. It was his paw to be sure. There was no doubt about that. He saw his paws every day. Why they now seemed alien to him, as alien as the hideous face in the water, the beast did not know.

He looked at the monster face staring back at him from the pond water and made a mournful sound. The face in the water matched his paws. So, why did it come as such a shock to him to discover what his face looked like? It was a puzzle to the mutant beast. He thought hard, or as hard as he was able, anyway, but, no solution came to him.

What should his face look like, he pondered, if not like the one in the water? An image flickered behind the monster's eyes, the image of a face, a human face – the face of a thin boy with dark, messy hair, a narrow chin and large eyes made larger still by the thick, unbecoming glasses that he wore. Was this his true face?

The monster was confused. Why should he have a human face? He knew he was different from humans – *very* different. Then why should he imagine that his face ought to be a human one? He could make nothing of it in his dim, troglodyte brain.

With an angry growl, the monster slashed at the image in the water with his huge claws, throwing up a geyser of white spray and sending most of the animals at the pond scurrying for the safety of the bushes.

Suddenly, a whole flurry of images poured into the creature's troubled brain – familiar faces, the boys, a man's and a woman's – all faces he knew, but only vaguely.

The behemoth rose, cupped a paw over his cat's eyes, then staggered back and fell into the great oak that grew near the water's edge. The whole tree shook with the force of the impact with his iron body. Birds nesting in the boughs above all took flight at once in a fury of beating wings and frightened, angry chirps and leaves showered down like rain around the monster.

The mutant beast huddled there at the base of the tree, his ugly head cradled in his vast paws, eyes squeezed shut, as images and memories besieged his muddled brain.

He saw the boy; the boy with the face he thought was his own, sitting at a table in a grubby little house. He was happily eating dinner with the man and the woman. They were talking, enjoying themselves.

He saw the man and the boy in what looked like a back alley, tossing a ball back and forth, smiling and laughing. He saw the boy, much younger this time, crying, his knee bloody. But the woman was there, holding the boy, caressing him, tending to his injured knee.

Then, they were all in a car together – *the* car – driving through a lonely desert. At first all seemed all right, but then, ahead of them, rocks tumbled suddenly down the mountainside. The man turned the car too sharply and it plunged over the edge of a ravine and careened unceasingly down the slope.

The back door, somehow, flung open and the boy was thrown from the car. There was pain then, terrible, throbbing pain, and his mind spiraled into darkness.

He came to only for a brief moment, unable to move. But he could see the car, crumpled and ruined and surrounded by a raging fire. And he could hear the woman screaming, screaming for her life. The screams drilled into the boy's brain just as it again sank into a womb of darkness.

The monster scrambled to his feet, shaking his great head angrily, trying to dispel the horrid images inside it.

At last, the mutant titan let out a tremendous roar that echoed throughout the whole of Brush Canyon, doubled his huge paw into an iron-hard fist, and lashed out with the force of a bomb blast. The mighty fist struck the great oak and the trunk shattered as if hit with a missile. The whole seventy foot tree came crashing down in the glen, sending up a shower of leaves and broken branches as it hit. What few animals remained in the bushes near the pond scattered then – fleeing for the safety of the hills above.

The mutant goliath stood there then, steam billowing from his gnarled knuckles, and looked around bewilderedly at the outcome of his horrific outburst. He watched wretchedly as the animals fled, then looked down at the devastated oak.

It had once stood so proudly in the glen – a grandfather of an oak, home to squirrels, and birds, and shade to other beasts, the monster too at times, during the desert heat of the day. The old tree had been a fixture in the glen, probably as old as the canyon itself.

Now, it lay shattered and in ruins, little more than fireplace kindling, thanks to the mutant's swift, thoughtless handiwork. The monster stood gaping, sadly, stupidly and remorsefully – what else could he do?

At that moment, he heard a tiny, pained squeak nearby, and his rubbery, wolfish ears perked up amid his shaggy, black mane. He glanced down at a large section of the trunk of the felled tree and spotted a bushy, gray tail protruding from beneath it. He reached down, hefted the trunk, and tossed it away.

There on the ground, gasping its last painful breaths, was a squirrel. It breathed rapidly and with a slight gurgle as blood came into its throat. The monster grimaced, then, as gently as his huge claws would permit, he reached down and scooped up the mortally wounded little creature. He held it close to his face, watching it hopefully, but, to no avail.

The squirrel gave a few last kicks and shudders, then its little, gray body went limp and its moist, black eyes grew cloudy and blank.

The atomic monster trembled. A great mournful sadness came over him and he sank to his knees. He held the tiny, lifeless body close to his face. If he had had tear ducts, he would have wept for the dead creature. He had killed it with his great anger and greater clumsiness. Even with his dim mind, he knew this and regretted it.

With a heavy, hollow heart, he scooped up a claw full of earth, laid the small, limp body in the hole, and sprinkled the dirt over it. He didn't know why he did this – some dormant instinct made the act compulsory.

After a moment of mourning over the tiny grave, the radioactive behemoth rose, gave a last sad look at the glen, then trudged back up the slope toward the lonely hills above.

Chapter - 7

Professor Willoughby sighed sadly and sank back against the sofa, his heart laden with guilt. He had told everything he knew to his enemies in the hope of saving his young visitors, and to stall for much needed time. But, he feared he'd done all this in vain.

Surely, these villains planned to kill them all in the end to keep them from talking. But, any scheme a man could cling to, the professor reasoned, was worth the effort on the off chance that it might work.

Sitting on the sofa next to him, Skip and Johnny were both looking lost and forlorn. Betty Jo, her blue eyes glazed with tears, was standing beside them with Petrovich's meaty hand on her shoulder, a look of utter desolation marring her lovely features.

Across from them, in the professor's easy chair, perched a much placated Von Kepler, his bony legs crossed, his gloved fingers laced, a thin, satisfied grin stretched across his cadaverous face.

"I must thank you adamantly, Alfred, for the information," he said at length. "You have been most cooperative. Your account was very detailed and precise. Thinking of trailing the beast with a Geiger counter was sheer genius – so simple that even I didn't think of it. However, I have no time to utilize such a crude method this evening. I am anxious, you understand, to be done with this business as soon as possible."

Von Kepler stood up. "With that in mind, I have decided that one of you will lead me to this old quarry pit you described. The rest will remain here until I have verified all you have told me."

"After that, if all goes as planned and you have spoken truly, I will release you all and take my leave." Von Kepler's cruel face darkened then. "However, if even one word you have told me proves to be false, not one of you will leave this house alive."

Betty Jo gasped audibly, which brought a fresh smile to the Nazi's wicked face.

"I've told you the truth, Heinrich," declared the professor as he rose from the sofa. "And I'll lead you to the cave. You may as well let the children go, now. They're of no further use to you."

"I think not," Von Kepler said flatly. He gestured and Petrovich aimed his pistol at the old man's chest. "Sit down, Willoughby. I will choose my own guide, thank you." He glanced at Miroff. "Tie the three of them up," he commanded.

As Miroff produced a coil of rope from his coat and approached the sofa, Von Kepler turned toward Betty Jo. He gave an oily grin as he sauntered up to the frightened girl. "I think the pretty girl shall lead us to the cave," he proclaimed casually. "You do know the area well, my dear. You told me so yourself, if you recall."

Betty Jo fervently wished that she had kept her mouth shut, but it was too late, now, to deny what she'd said. "Yes, I do," she confessed reluctantly.

"And you have been to this cave before?"

"Yes," Betty Jo said quietly. "I used to play in it when we first moved here."

"Fine," said Von Kepler as he gave an ugly grin. "Then I have picked my guide wisely."

As Miroff was tying his arms, the professor glowered at the Nazi. "Leave that child out of this, Von Kepler!" he snarled. "She received a head wound in that smash-up tonight! Her condition is too delicate to have her traipsing through the canyon in the middle of the night!"

Von Kepler kept his goggled eyes focused on Betty Jo. "You would prefer I took the little boy instead?"

Betty Jo's blue eyes went wide with fright. "*No!*" she shrieked. "Please! I'll go. I know right where it is!"

"No, Betty Jo!" Johnny shouted while rope was wound around his arms, pinning them to his sides. "I'll go! I know the canyon lots better than you do! I go there all the time with Billy and Chuck. Besides, you're a *girl*!"

"What about this fat one?" Petrovich suggested as he cinched rope tightly around Skip's meaty arms.

The plump boy winced and felt faint. He wanted to volunteer, but he couldn't find the courage to speak up.

Von Kepler snickered. "That thick-bodied lout? I doubt he could walk more than a few meters before giving out with exhaustion. Besides, he is obviously a spineless coward. What man with an ounce of courage would sit idly by while a woman and a child offered themselves up so readily?"

He glanced back at Betty Jo. "No, the girl is the best choice." He put a gloved finger under Betty Jo's bowed chin and lifted her face, then wiped the tears from her pink cheeks with his thumb. "She not only has courage, but beauty as well. And the others will not dare to defy me so long as she is with me."

Betty Jo shrank away from the Nazi, a look of disgust and hatred twisting her pretty face.

On the sofa, now tightly bound, Skip felt about as useless as anyone could feel. Von Kepler's cruel words had struck him right in the heart. Worse still were the looks he'd received from Betty Jo and Johnny.

From Johnny, the look had been one of disdain, which was bad enough. But, Betty Jo had given him a look of pity – which was even worse. Skip wasn't sure he could ever live this episode down, assuming, that is, that he lived at all!

With Johnny and the two men safely bound on the sofa, the two big Russians turned to Von Kepler for instructions. "They are secure, Doctor," said Petrovich. "Shall we tie the girl as well?"

"No, fool," Von Kepler balked. "How can she lead us through the canyon if she's wound up in rope?" He pointed at Petrovich. "You will remain here to guard the men," he ordered. "Watch Willoughby closely. He is a crafty Englishman."

"Yes, Doctor," said Petrovich.

Von Kepler turned to Miroff. "You will come along with me to the canyon to handle the girl."

Miroff merely nodded. He refused to waste words on the Nazi. He moved up behind Betty Jo and laid a gloved hand gently on her shoulder.

The forlorn teenager glanced up at him with damp, melancholy eyes. Miroff smiled slightly down at her, trying to reassure her, but she turned her face away from him just as a tear rolled down her swollen, pink cheek.

Miroff sighed inwardly. He hated doing what he was doing, but he had no choice. He was an agent of the KGB, and he had a mission to complete. He knew he had to do his duty to the Kremlin, regardless of his personal feelings.

Still, he couldn't bring himself to harden his heart against this lovely girl – not when she so resembled his beloved little sister, Katrina. This would complicate matters when it came time to liquidate the poor girl. The thought of it tormented the big Russian, but his orders from his superiors were quite clear – no witnesses.

Miroff hated war, especially cold ones. At least a hot war offered open battle – an honorable conflict between men. This odious Cold War was fought in secret and in a cowardly, inhuman fashion with killers and victims instead of warriors. It was a disgrace for a fighting man like himself. But, it was the reality he had no choice but to face.

Miroff hoped that, when it came time to do away with the girl, he would be spared the task and that the Nazi would pull the trigger himself. He could then, at least, avenge the young beauty by giving the Nazi the same treatment. That was one order from the Kremlin he would have little trouble carrying out.

"All right," Von Kepler began, "we waste no more time. We leave for the canyon, now." He stepped in front of the sofa and regarded the professor and the two boys through his dark goggles.

"I would wish me luck for your sake, Alfred," said the Nazi coolly. "I had best not return here empty handed, or things will not go pleasantly for the three of you."

Professor Willoughby met the German's goggled eyes stoically. "Heinrich, I beseech you for the last time. Leave that child here and take me along with you."

"You needn't concern yourself with the little girl's safety, Englander," Von Kepler replied flatly. "So long as she tries no tricks, no harm will come to her. Your own neck is in far greater peril than is hers, old man."

Von Kepler's voice suddenly turned icy and malevolent. "Do you remember how you gloated when you were given leave to shut down my project?" he snarled. "Well, now it is *my* turn to gloat! Shortly, the dream of Herr Hitler will finally be realized – a super-race of German making will walk the earth!"

Professor Willoughby's beetle-black eyes narrowed behind his rectangular spectacles. "They have a saying here in the colonies, Heinrich," he declared in a quiet voice. "Don't count your chickens before they've hatched."

"Bah!" Von Kepler scoffed and waved a hand dismissively. "I have no more time to waste on you!" He turned to Betty Jo. "Fräulein, you will now lead us to the cave," he commanded coldly. "I must warn you, any attempt to escape, or to trick us shall be dealt with very harshly! Do you understand?"

Betty Jo nodded hopelessly. "Yes."

"Good." Von Kepler gestured to Miroff. "Take her to the car," he ordered.

The tall Russian took Betty Jo's shoulders and guided her quietly out of the room.

The Nazi turned and faced the professor and the two boys once more. "I give all of you one last warning as well," he said crisply. "I am leaving you in the hands of Comrade Petrovich. You will try no foolishness while we are gone or, I promise you, he will certainly shoot you."

Without further comment, the German turned on his heel and stormed out of the room after Miroff and Betty Jo.

When the Nazi had gone, Petrovich, gun drawn, sauntered over to the professor's armchair and eased his considerable bulk into it. He aimed his pistol straight at the professor's heart and made himself comfortable. He kept his deep-set, black eyes trained constantly on the elderly Englishman.

The professor glared right back, unafraid and defiant.

Beside the old man, Skip was sweating buckets as he stared at the muzzle of the Russian's automatic. He could feel his heart hammering in his chest and it was all he could do to keep from fainting dead away.

He had never been this afraid in all his seventeen years, not even when confronted by the *Wheel Cats*, a local gang of hotrod thugs led by the tough, bullying Tony Moran.

Moran and his thugs might rough him up, Skip mused darkly, but this communist creep was likely to kill him, kill them all, to keep them from talking about what had transpired here tonight.

In fact, Skip could visualize no other outcome. These villains were not merely a band of cheap crooks; they were deadly, professional agents – killers with a license. Men like that did not leave loose ends when they did a job, and he, the Carlsons and the old professor definitely qualified as loose ends. That meant that none of them would leave this house alive.

The mere thought caused Skip to start shaking. A tear leaked from one eye. He couldn't help it. He hoped Johnny hadn't seen it. He glanced at the boy to be sure, but Johnny wasn't looking at him.

Johnny, in fact, was crying, too, and his little round face was pink and desolate.

Skip wished he could reassure the kid, but that was impossible. Even if he weren't tied up, he had nothing to say to the boy that might comfort him. Truth be told, he could have used a little comfort himself. It looked very much like they were all going to be shot that night, and there was nothing they could do to escape it.

Chapter – 8

The big, green Buick sedan trundled silently along the canyon road as the moon hung in the night sky above like a great silver eye, spying on the desert land below and the sinister events that transpired there.

Miroff drove while Von Kepler and the captive Betty Jo rode together in the back seat.

The teenager's pretty face was swollen, pink and damp from the tears that just kept falling in spite of the girl's best efforts to hold them back.

Betty Jo had gone past terrified and was now in a paralytic, accepting stage. She sat beside the wicked German looking vague and morose, her spirit broken. She was going to die tonight, so were Johnny and the others, and there was nothing anyone could do to prevent it.

Her mind had accepted her fate and so her manner was almost serene. All thought of escape had been long abandoned. All hope had shriveled the moment she got in the car, and so she sat, desolate but at peace, in the back seat with her kidnapper. What else, after all, could she do?

Miroff glanced in the rearview mirror and spotted the hopeless, despondent look on Betty Jo's face and felt a pang of guilt flare up in his chest. She was little more than a child, this young beauty, yet she looked a hundred years old as she sat there, broken by despair, her sea-blue eyes glazed over and dull like the eyes of a dying animal.

The big Russian turned his attention back to the road. He couldn't bear to look at the poor girl anymore. In her mind, she was dead already. All that remained there in the back seat of the Buick was a husk – a lovely, but inanimate shell, no more alive than a rag doll.

Only Von Kepler seemed to be in good spirits. He glanced at the pretty girl beside him and gave an oily grin. "Don't look so melancholy, my dear," he said snidely. "This business will all be over shortly, and you'll be home and snug in your bed. Do try and endure that long, if you please."

Betty Jo looked at the Nazi, unbelieving. "Do you really mean that?"

Von Kepler shrugged. "But, of course," he trilled. "Why would I lie? How would it possibly benefit me?"

Betty Jo narrowed her eyes. "I'll be easier to handle if I'm calm," she pointed out.

"You are calm already," the German observed.

"I'm in shock," Betty Jo replied knowingly. "You know that. You also know it would be dangerous for you to leave any of us alive."

Von Kepler didn't answer, and his eyes were unreadable behind the dark goggles.

"Will you promise me one thing?" Betty Jo pleaded. "Will you spare little Johnny? He's only a child. Will you promise me that much?"

"I will promise you only one thing, little girl," the Nazi said coldly, "I will throttle him with my own hands if you fail me."

Betty Jo turned her face away from the German and back to the window. She watched the night-shrouded desert landscape go by quietly. Her last hope to save her dear little brother had been in vain.

Now, with all hope faded away, she had no reason to keep communicating with the vile monster in the seat beside her. She closed her eyes and muttered a prayer for Johnny. At least, she could do that much for him. Anything else was in the hands of a higher power.

Petrovich yawned, leaned back in the professor's easy chair and laid his pistol in his lap. He glanced at his wristwatch. It was 11:30. It had been a long day and he was weary.

He and Miroff had arrived on an early flight from West Germany, and had been met at the airport by Von Kepler. They had rented a car and driven from San Diego right away, stopping only once to eat at a miserable roadside diner. He had eaten nothing since then, and his big belly was reminding him of this fact at regular intervals.

Across from Petrovich on the sofa, Professor Willoughby was eyeing the burly Russian keenly – waiting for an opportunity to bait him into a trap.

"Tell me something, comrade," the professor taunted, "does it make you feel brave? Bullying children and an old man? Is that how the Kremlin gets its kicks these days?"

Petrovich sneered dispassionately at the professor. "I am a soldier," he said without emotion. "I only follow orders."

"Oh, that's a handy dodge!" balked the professor. "The Nazis claimed the same thing after the war. Remember?"

"I know," confessed the Russian. "I fought them. I was with the Red Army when we liberated Berlin."

Professor Willoughby's eyes narrowed. "Then you know damn well better than to be cooperating with one of them now!"

Petrovich yawned again. "That war is over," he reasoned. "This is a new war. The Nazis are not our enemies this time. *You* are."

"Oh, bosh! That's a load of tommyrot and you know it!" bellowed the professor. "The Cold War is nothing more than a dismal hoax on the whole world! It's a colossal con job, and you've fallen for it! And so have those simple-minded bosses of yours in Moscow!"

Petrovich shrugged. "I've fallen for nothing," he said casually. "I am a soldier, like I said. Not a politician. I follow orders."

"Even if those orders mean killing innocent civilians?" the professor challenged. "Children to boot? What of your soldier's honor?"

"To a soldier, duty comes first," said Petrovich. "His duty may not always be pleasant, but it is his duty all the same."

"Bloody convenient duty!" snapped the professor bitterly.

"No more talk," Petrovich declared as he held up a gloved hand. Presently, he stood up. "I hunger, Englishman. Where do you keep your food?"

"In the kitchen of course, you blasted nincompoop!" the old man growled. "It's just through that door and to the left."

Petrovich bent and examined the knots that bound his three hostages. Then, satisfied that they were secure, he regarded the professor. "I am going to get something to eat. You three sit still and keep quiet. Try no tricks, understand?"

"We aren't deaf, you know," barked the professor. "And don't mess up the kitchen while you're helping yourself to my food!"

The Russian ignored the dig and headed for the doorway. There, he paused a moment and gave his prisoners a cold stare. "Remember what I said. No tricks! I have very good hearing."

"Indeed!" the professor sniped.

A moment later, the big Russian had gone from the parlor, leaving the professor and the two boys alone in the room. The old scientist saw his chance. He glanced at Skip and Johnny.

"All right, lads, this is our shot and it may be our *only* one! Let's make it count! Let's see if we can do anything with these knots." He began to tug and heave on the ropes that bound him.

"It's no use, Prof," Skip said hopelessly. "They're too tight. We can't get loose."

Johnny shot Skip a wicked glare. "Aw, shut up, fat-chicken!"

"Now, now, boys," the professor scolded. "Try to work together. Our lives, as well as Miss Carlson's, depend on our escaping."

They all began to squirm against their bonds, but to no avail. Then, the professor thought of something. He looked at Johnny. "Johnny, are you in the Boy Scouts?" he asked.

"No," Johnny admitted. "I'm in the *Rural Rangers*! The Rangers are way better than the dumb ol' Boy Scouts!"

"Fine," said the professor. "Better enough that you always carry a pocket knife in case of emergencies?"

Johnny's blue eyes lit up. "Sure, I carry a pocket knife," he gushed. "A *Kamp King*! Best knife you can get! It's got a bottle opener, a screwdriver, a can opener, and everything!"

"We'll only need the blade," the professor assured him. "Hopefully, it's a sharp one. See if you can reach it."

"You bet, Prof!" Johnny began to squirrel around in the ropes, trying to reach the back pocket of his dungarees. But, with the cruel hemp cinched so tightly around his small body, it was tough going.

Skip watched him tensely for a few moments, his trepidation growing with each passing second. "Hurry up, will you kid?" he groused. "Before Comrade Karloff comes back and catches you!"

"Aw, zip your lip, tubby!" Johnny growled angrily. He'd always despised Skip's craven nature, and now it proved especially tiresome. Johnny managed to wriggle his small hand behind him enough to reach the pocket, but the tough denim was too taut to permit his fingers to delve very deeply inside.

Johnny grunted and squirmed. Finally, he leaned to one side, which loosened the material just enough that he was able to deftly slither his small fingers into the pocket enough to clasp the knife.

Getting the knife out of the pocket, however, proved more difficult still. With his fingers clenched around the hilt, it was impossible for Johnny to withdraw his hand. The child grunted and tugged as much as he dared, but to no avail.

"Haven't you got it yet?" Skip hissed in a fright.

"I can't," Johnny despaired. "I can't pull it out! The pocket's too tight!"

"Great!" Skip groaned. "Just great!"

"Shut up, will you!" snapped the professor. He turned to Johnny. "You're all bunched up," he pointed out. "Try to straighten out your right leg a little. That ought to release some of the tension on the fabric. Then, you can pull out the knife."

"Okay, Professor," Johnny said obediently. He did as he was told, and, just as the old man had said, the fabric loosened and the knife came out in his hand. "I've got it!"

"About time!" Skip grumbled.

"Stick a cork in it!" Johnny shot back as he straightened up, knife in hand.

"All right, enough bickering," the professor chided. "Remember, lads, Miss Carlson is counting on us to keep our heads."

He turned to Johnny. "Now, listen to me closely, my boy. Pull the blade out as carefully as you can. Slip it under the rope around your chest near the knot and start sawing. Remember to keep the blade turned away from your body at all times. Understand?"

"Sure, Prof," said Johnny. The seven-year-old gulped quietly and brought his small hands together. He grasped the raised area on the longest blade of the camp knife and slid a fingernail into the groove notched in it. Then, using all his concentration, Johnny slowly pulled open the shining blade. After what seemed like a very long time, the blade finally clicked into position.

"I got it!" Johnny chirped. "It's open!"

"Excellent!" exclaimed the professor. "Now, go to work on those ropes, lad. And be careful not to cut yourself."

"Yes, sir!" Johnny brought the knife up to his sternum and, with painstaking caution, slid the blade between the rope and his soft chest. He could feel the back of the blade biting into his tender flesh and knew that, if the blade slipped sideways, he might very well cut himself badly.

Sweat formed on the child's brow as he sawed slowly on the thick rope. It would take time to saw through it, perhaps too much time, but, with his limited strength, it couldn't be helped.

Skip was sweating too, as he watched with bated breath. Every second that ticked away on the grandfather's clock in the corner behind them sounded to him like the cocking of a pistol hammer.

He knew that, at any moment, the big Russian might come barging back into the parlor and catch them in the act of trying to escape.

What would the Russian do? Would he bother simply taking the knife away and giving the kid a swift belt? Or, would he just start slinging lead? Skip had no desire to find out.

"Hurry up, will you? That goon won't be in the kitchen all night, for Pete's sake!"

"Don't rush the boy!" the professor snapped. "If that blade slips he might very well slice an artery!"

"Oh yeah?" Skip hissed. "Well, if that Commie comes back and catches him, he might wind up full of holes! And so will the rest of us!"

"Shut up, *damn* you!" the old man snarled. He turned back to Johnny. "Just keep concentrating, Johnny," he advised. "Block out everything else and focus on that one spot on the rope."

"Yes, sir," Johnny said, and he kept on sawing, his eyes and mind focused on the rhythmic motion of the blade. The rope was already half through. In another few moments, he'd be free. He had to concentrate. He could almost hear Skip sweating on the sofa next to him.

The tick of the big clock started to sound like footsteps. Even the professor's labored breathing became a distraction. But Johnny kept sawing away, minute after fretful minute.

Then, after a sudden snap and the merciful release of the rigorous tension around his body, the rope cut through. "I did it!" Johnny exclaimed, excited. He shrugged and wriggled and the scratchy, clutching hemp coils fell away from his body. He rubbed his numb, tingling arms until life began to pour back into them.

"Good lad!" praised the professor. "Now, cut us free before our friend in the kitchen finishes his meal."

"Yes, sir!" Johnny chirped. He went to work on the professor's bindings first. It was much quicker going this time because his hands and arms were no longer restricted.

In just a few moments, the old man was standing beside Johnny, shaking off the cut ropes like a snake shedding its skin.

"Give me the knife, Johnny," the professor commanded. "I'll cut our fat friend free while you keep an eye out for that communist hooligan."

"Okay, Prof," Johnny said as he surrendered his camp knife. "But, if I was you, I'd just leave Skip tied up. He'll only be in the way."

Skip glared at Johnny as the professor worked to cut him free. "Just remember who saved your bacon tonight, pipsqueak," he grumbled. "I could have left you lay out there by the gully!"

From the doorway where he'd stationed himself to keep watch, Johnny stuck his tongue out at the plump teenager.

"That'll do, lads" the professor chided as he cut through and removed Skip's bindings. "Remember, we must work together if we're to defeat those villains and rescue Miss Carlson."

Once the ropes were off, Skip stood and rubbed life back into his numb limbs. "Just how do you plan to do all this?" he demanded of the professor. "They all have guns. All we've got is a crummy scout knife."

The professor tapped his bald cranium. "By using our brains over their brawn," he confided. "Now, follow me to the kitchen." He gestured. "It's this way."

Skip sighed and swallowed the lump of fright which had swollen rapidly in his throat. He was beginning to wish he'd called the sheriff the moment he'd spotted Betty Jo's car burning in the gully and let him deal with the whole mess.

It would have been the smartest, safest solution for almost all of them. Had he done that, Betty Jo and Johnny would've been taken to the hospital in San Bolero, where they'd be right now, safe and sound, and he would be at home in bed, where he belonged.

As he trailed behind the eccentric old Brit and the rambunctious seven-year-old, it occurred to Skip that he might well be heading to his doom. But, when he thought of Betty Jo, still in the clutches of that Nazi madman, the danger to him seemed secondary.

Somehow, the fat boy mused, he'd have to muddle through this and make, at least, some small contribution to the mutual efforts of his compatriots. If he did, it might finally earn him the respect, and perhaps even the love, of the girl of his dreams.

In the kitchen, KGB agent Petrovich sat at the small, round kitchen table, munching on a ham sandwich and sipping a cup of hot coffee. He was content for the first time since he'd arrived in California. The mission was going well.

Miroff, his able partner, was already on his way to the cave to subdue the animal, or whatever it was, and to do away with their Nazi collaborator. When Miroff returned, it would be a simple matter to dispose of the remaining witnesses, bury their bodies in the desert, and be at the rendezvous point at the beach with the creature in plenty of time to meet the submarine.

No doubt their superiors at the Kremlin would be ecstatic over such a coup, and reward them both with promotions and plenty of kudos. Failure at this point seemed ludicrous. In fact, this had been one of their easier assignments of late.

He and Miroff had primarily been assigned to kidnap and assassinate foreign dignitaries, or to do counterintelligence work against the British MI6 and American CIA – missions with plenty of pitfalls and danger, and they had both risked their lives many times for Mother Russia.

This assignment, as strange as it was, didn't present nearly the degree of peril that Petrovich and Miroff were used to, and, as such, seemed more like a pleasant, California vacation.

Secretly, Petrovich was almost sorry this mission would only last a day or two. He had always wanted to visit a California beach and see all the pretty girls clad in their revealing bathing suits. Sights like that were very rare in his home in Siberia. In fact, they didn't exist there.

But, they were due to meet the sub by night, and no one would be on the beach at night. He would have to be content to enjoy the warm weather for a bit longer and the American food. Petrovich took another bite of his ham sandwich and grinned as he chewed. It might not be gourmet cuisine, but it was better than cold potato soup any day of the week.

Professor Willoughby and the two boys, meanwhile, quietly approached the kitchen from the connecting hallway. The professor was leading the way, while Skip took up the rear.

Skip was sweating buckets and wishing he were someplace else. When the old man paused in the doorway, the teenager decided it was high time to act on his fears.

"Hey," he hissed to the professor, "let's get out of here while the getting is good! We can round up the sheriff and a few deputies and clean this whole mess up in twenty minutes!"

"No," snapped the professor. "We'd be too late by then to save Miss Carlson. We must act here and now!"

"We're liable to get our heads blown off here and now!" Skip protested. "Then who'd save Betty Jo?"

"Aw, turn blue, fat-chicken!" Johnny spat disgustedly. "Go ahead and run out on us! The Prof and me can do it without you!"

"Do what, pee-wee?" Skip demanded. "Get shot?"

Johnny doubled up his small fist and aimed a punch at Skip's ample middle, but the professor caught the blow before it connected.

"Boys, please!" he pleaded. "We can't afford to quarrel amongst ourselves! Miss Carlson's life hangs in the balance! We mustn't lose heart now. Besides, we can't bring the sheriff into this without upsetting the whole applecart. We must do it ourselves!"

Skip's eyes narrowed and he glared at the old professor. "So, that's why you're so anxious!" he growled. "It's not Betty Jo you're thinking of at all! You're thinking of that damn monster of yours!"

"I'm thinking of them both, Walters," the professor shot back. "Don't you realize what will happen if Von Kepler gets his hands on that poor brute? He'll use his radioactive cells to breed a superhuman mutant army! An undefeatable army! Can't you see what such an army would do in his hands? Or in the hands of the Soviet Union?"

For the first time, Skip got a grip on himself. Now that he realized what was at stake, his much imbued patriotism surfaced again and served to overwhelm his fears – for the time being. "Okay, okay," he finally relented.

"All right, let's go to it, then," said the professor, and he continued down the hallway, this time with both boys close behind him. A moment later, they were standing just outside the doorway to the kitchen.

Sitting at the kitchen table was the communist agent, Petrovich, blithely munching away on a ham sandwich and wholly oblivious to their presence. His automatic pistol rested on the table beside him, along with his gloves and dark gray fedora.

The professor motioned for the two boys to stop. "There the rascal is," whispered the old man. "Keep as quiet as possible."

Johnny and Skip both nodded.

As quietly as he could, Professor Willoughby tip-toed into the kitchen behind the Russian and opened one of the overhead cabinets. After a bit of rummaging, his hand emerged from the cabinet clasping a sturdy, wooden rolling pin. He turned to the two boys, who were still lingering in the doorway, and gave them a wink as he brandished the rolling pin like a club.

Johnny clasped a small hand over his mouth to suppress a giggle, while Skip ran a thick finger around the collar of his shirt to loosen it.

At the table, Petrovich sat munching away; still unaware he was being plotted against only a few feet behind him.

The professor proceeded to creep up on his unsuspecting adversary, the rolling pin held high and ready to strike. At last, when he judged himself to be within sufficient distance to deliver an effective blow, the professor raised the wooden bludgeon as high as he could get it, and then brought it down with all the force his aged limbs could muster.

There was a loud crack as the rolling pin connected with the big Russian's skull. Petrovich swayed in his chair for an instant, and then dropped like a stone to the kitchen floor.

"Take that, you gluttonous ruffian!" shouted the professor triumphantly as he stood proudly over the felled communist.

Johnny and Skip hurried into the kitchen. "Boy, that was swell, Professor!" chirped Johnny. "You're a regular spy-smasher!"

"Indeed," the professor remarked with subdued modesty. He picked up the unconscious Russian's pistol from the table and pulled back the slide, cocking it. "That's one fiend down. Just two more to go."

The old man indicated Petrovich. "Johnny, hurry back to the parlor and fetch some of that rope. We have to tie this scoundrel up before he comes to."

"Yes, sir!" chimed Johnny, and he rushed away to do as he was told.

Skip rolled the Russian onto his belly and pulled his hands behind his back so they could be tied. "I can't believe I'm doing this," he observed.

"Believe it, young Walters," said the professor as he pocketed the pistol. "And be prepared to do still more. We have a stiff fight ahead of us, I fear."

"Swell," Skip gulped in reply.

Johnny came back in a flash with a coil of rope and handed it to Skip. Then, the two of them began tying up the unconscious communist while the professor donned his heavy, tweed frock coat. When they were finished, the two boys stood up.

"All done, Prof," Johnny announced. "He ain't going anywhere."

"Isn't," corrected the professor. "That's fine, lads. We'll have the sheriff collect that Bolshevik hoodlum after we've dealt with the others."

"I still think we ought to call the sheriff now," Skip insisted. "Sure, we conked this goof when his back was turned, but that Nazi guy isn't so stupid. We're liable to be walking right into a hornet's nest if we go chasing him into that old quarry pit alone."

"We have two advantages over Von Kepler," the professor pointed out. "The first is what you Yanks call *home field advantage*. By that I mean that we know that old quarry cave better than he does. Our second advantage, and this one is crucial, is the element of surprise. The Germans are an egotistical lot. They were that way in both wars, which is part of the reason they lost."

"Von Kepler has underestimated our resourcefulness. He'll never suspect that we bested his crony and escaped. Nor would he ever dream that we'd pursue and confront him alone if we did. That, I assure you, will come as a complete surprise to him."

"Even so," Skip protested, "the sheriff and his deputies are the pros at this sort of stuff. They could handle those two creeps way better than we could."

"Aw, stay here if you're chicken!" Johnny sniped disgustedly.

"Actually, you're wrong, Walters," the professor proclaimed. "That nincompoop sheriff doesn't know Von Kepler as I do. He could easily bungle the operation and get poor Miss Carlson killed. No, you must trust me. We have to do this ourselves."

Skip looked hesitant. He had no wish for harm to come to Betty Jo, but the fear inside him had the strength of Hercules. It was all the boy could do to back it down.

Finally, he sighed. "Okay," he relented. "What's the worst that could happen? I get killed?"

"That's the spirit, my lad!" said the professor heartily. He slapped Skip on the shoulder, then turned and crossed to the cabinets. He opened a drawer and pulled out a large flashlight. "We'll need a torch," he said as he faced the boys. "Now, follow me, lads! We have villains to thwart and a fair maiden to rescue!"

"You bet, Professor!" cheered Johnny.

With that, the professor hurried out of the kitchen with Johnny hot on his heels.

Skip lingered a moment, shaking his head, then trailed reluctantly behind the others. "I'm gonna regret this," he muttered to himself on the way out the door. "I know I am."

The professor led the boys down the hallway to a locked door at the end. He produced a set of keys from the pocket of his frock coat, unlocked the door, and hurried into the room beyond. The boys followed him closely.

"This is the garage," the old man announced as he flipped on a light. Parked in the garage, taking up most of the room, in fact, was a large military vehicle.

Skip and Johnny stood gaping. "Golly, it's an army truck!" Johnny observed excitedly. "Neat-o!"

"It's a troop carrier," the professor said as they approached the big vehicle. "I needed a vehicle like this to transport our monstrous friend in the canyon. He weighs as much as ten men. I also needed something with a canopy to hide what I was transporting."

"Where did you get it, Prof?" Johnny asked.

"I stole it, of course," the professor confessed unabashed. "From Project Omega."

"Oh, that's great," Skip grumbled as they all climbed into the cab. "You're not only wanted for harboring a monster, they're also after you for grand theft auto!"

"Don't be such a dramatist," the professor said as he shut the driver's side door. "We, as they say, have bigger fish to fry."

The old man put the key in the ignition, turned it, and the big motor roared to life. "All right," the professor shouted over the din and rattle of the engine. "The game is afoot! Tally ho!" He threw the truck into gear, stepped on the gas pedal and the troop carrier rumbled into motion.

"Hey, Prof," Skip jabbered in alarm, "you forgot to open the garage doors!"

"So I did," said the professor, unperturbed. He accelerated and the truck smashed through the wooden garage doors, reducing them to kindling. "Needed new garage doors, anyway!"

Skip and Johnny exchanged a shocked glance as the truck bounced along the bumpy driveway, heading for the canyon road.

Chapter – 9

Miroff pulled the big, green Buick off the road onto the shoulder and parked it near a narrow path that wound back into the canyon. He shut off the motor and glanced back at Von Kepler.

"You're certain this is the spot, child?" the German asked Betty Jo.

"Yes," the blonde girl replied. "If we follow that trail, it will lead us straight to Ghost Rock Cave."

Von Kepler climbed out of the car and pulled Betty Jo out after him. He waited until Miroff was out of the car, and then regarded the teenager. "You lead the way, girl," he commanded. "And remember – there will be a gun pointed at your back the whole time. I advise you not to try running, or anything foolish."

Betty Jo merely glanced miserably at the two men, then turned and started off down the dusty trail.

The rugged path through the canyon to the old quarry pit would be rough going for Betty Jo in her long skirt, crinolines, and low-heeled wicker pumps, but she knew her captors would care little about her comfort.

She made up her mind not to mention it, no matter how bad it got. She was determined not to give these barbarians the satisfaction of knowing she was uncomfortable. It would only add to her humiliation, and she had been humiliated enough for one night.

The trail started off relatively mild – merely a rock-strewn, dusty path, about seven feet wide, that wound meanderingly through the bushes and scattered boulders of the canyon.

At first, the path ran level, but, after about a quarter of a mile, it began to grade steeper and steeper as they went. The trail also became narrower and the bushes pressed in more, as did the branches of the odd tree. The rocks that littered the path were bigger the further along they got as well, and had to be dodged more frequently.

Even with Von Kepler's big, safari-type flashlight to light their way, Betty Jo still found herself stumbling over stones and other unseen encumbrances.

The big Russian, the one called Miroff, was always there to catch her when she fell and set her right again. When he caught her, he did so gently, so as not to harm her fragile body, and his hands never lingered on her inappropriately. It surprised the teenager that the Russian was something of a gentleman. Betty Jo began to feel that this man was not the monstrous oaf that she initially pegged him to be, but rather an old world warrior caught up in the hideous political turmoil of the times. A villain perhaps, she mused, but not one by choice. However, he was certainly in the wrong profession, and keeping very bad company.

It was the better part of a mile from the canyon road down to the ravine that contained the old quarry pit, and with Betty Jo stumbling so much due to her inadequate footwear, it was slow going. But, after a forty minute hike, Betty Jo and her captors finally came to the end of the trail. It stopped at the edge of the deep, bowl-shaped ravine where, years before, limestone had been extracted in great quantities to make driveway gravel.

At the bottom of the ravine, a number of large, cave-like holes dotted the craggy, irregular bluff face. The largest hole stood out from the others and had two hollows above it so that the jutting rock it occupied resembled a ghostly face. There was an old wooden sign posted at the opening, but, in the dark, it was unreadable at such a distance.

Betty Jo pointed. "That's it," she confirmed. "That's Ghost Rock Cave."

Von Kepler shone his light down into the ravine. The path leading into it was steep, narrow and treacherous. "You are certain?"

"Of course I am," snipped Betty Jo. "Like I told you, I used to play in it as a child. The quarry pit actually opens into a natural cavern further inside. The local kids all say it's haunted."

Von Kepler grinned sardonically. "They may be more right than they know," he observed. He gestured. "Let's go."

Betty Jo was about to lead the way, but Miroff caught her arm.

"She cannot make it down that steep ravine in those little shoes," he pointed out. "She'll stumble and fall."

"Then, carry her," Von Kepler commanded. He turned, then, and plunged down the steep path himself.

Miroff gently hoisted Betty Jo and settled her against his broad chest. He gave her a brief smile to dispel her fright, and then started down the steep, dusty grade with her held tight in his brawny arms. He kept a firm grip on the girl and shielded her body from the worst of the jostling as he negotiated his way down the slope. When he reached the bottom, he set Betty Jo down and smiled at her again. "You all right?" he asked.

Betty Jo nodded meekly. "Yes," she almost whispered.

Miroff smiled again and gestured.

Betty Jo followed behind Von Kepler, who led the way with his flashlight. They all stopped briefly at the mouth of the cave and glanced at the crude, wooden sign propped up there by a pile of stones. It read: KEEP OUT! The letters had been hastily scrawled in bright red paint which had dripped creepily. It looked as if it had been painted with fresh blood!

Von Kepler chuckled at the sign. "The work of children," he declared. He put away his flashlight and drew a small instrument from his trench coat pocket. He waved the instrument in front of the cave mouth, and then checked it. He smiled darkly.

"What is that?" Miroff asked.

"A dosimeter," Von Kepler replied. "Like a Geiger counter, it measures the presence of radiation. It will tell us whether Willoughby has lied to us in regard to the whereabouts of my creation."

"Well?"

Von Kepler pocketed the tool. "He was not lying," he confessed. "There is ionizing radiation here. The beast is in there at this very moment. Such a strong reaction couldn't be merely residual."

Miroff instinctively drew his pistol and began nervously scanning the terrain around them.

Von Kepler cackled rudely. "Put that plaything away, fool!" he chortled. "It will do you no good against him. Only I know how to subdue the beast. Keep that in mind, comrade."

"Miroff narrowed his eyes. "Yes, Doctor," he said bitterly. He put away his gun and guided Betty Jo into the mouth of the tunnel after the German.

They plodded into the gloomy pit with only the glow of Von Kepler's flashlight to illuminate the path before them. After a fairly short distance, the excavated portion of the tunnel gave way to the beauty of the natural cavern beyond. Above, stalactites stabbed down from the cave ceiling like tiger's fangs, while stalagmites vomited up from the slippery cavern floor to meet them in a menacing array.

Shortly, Betty Jo noticed a dim light with a blue-green hue emanating from all around them. The others noticed it too, and Von Kepler shut off his flashlight.

"Where does the light come from?" Miroff asked.

"It's *luminous algae*," Betty Jo informed him. "It grows on cave walls and gives off a faint light. As I recall, it's all over down here."

"Very astute observation, girl," Von Kepler admitted. "Clearly, you pay attention in your classes." Then he grinned scathingly. "Though, I never saw the point in educating a woman. You needn't know such things to rock a cradle."

Betty Jo glared at the Nazi, hating him.

"Our friend must be further inside," Von Kepler pointed out. "Come. Let's keep moving."

The procession started again. After a short distance, Betty Jo heard the faint rush of water ahead and knew they were approaching the underground river. The others heard it too, and they all paused.

"Water?" Miroff asked.

"Obviously," Von Kepler declared. He pointed with his flashlight. "It's coming from that direction."

"It's the underground river," said Betty Jo. "It runs all through the cave."

Von Kepler listened a moment. "He would choose a place to stay with a source of water," he observed vaguely. "We will find him close by. Come."

They kept on for a while, following the sound of the rushing water. Finally, they emerged in a large cavern filled with rich cave formations and lit from almost every side by the luminous algae.

They spotted a precipice ahead and approached it. Von Kepler peered over the edge and saw the black ribbon of rushing water some thirty feet below.

"There is our river," he declared. He came back to the others and looked around the cavern. Soon, he spotted a cave formation that overlooked the river where a stalactite and a stalagmite had merged together into a single post running from ceiling to floor. He pointed to it. "Tie the girl to that," he commanded.

Miroff glanced reluctantly at the teenager and nodded to her.

Betty Jo obediently approached the cave formation as Miroff produced a length of rope from inside his topcoat.

The Russian positioned Betty Jo against the cold, damp formation and deftly wound the rope around her body just beneath her breasts. He fastened the ends of the rope behind the formation, out of Betty Jo's reach, then came around and stood beside the frightened girl. He glanced at her, almost ashamed.

"I'm sorry," he told her honestly.

Tears were already welling in Betty Jo's blue eyes. Instinctively, she knew the end was near for her. She had led them through the canyon to the cave, and had now outlived her usefulness.

Her breast began to heave as her breathing became heavy. Sobs were wrenching at her insides and she struggled to hold them back. She didn't want Von Kepler to have the satisfaction of knowing he'd broken her.

Still, Betty Jo wasn't ready to die. She pleaded with the big Russian with her eyes – begged for mercy without words, but, sadly, he only turned his tormented face away from her. She could tell he felt guilty about what he was doing, but seemed bound by duty to see it through.

The teenager hung her head and wept. She knew for certain, now, that her time was at hand and that there was no escaping her fate. Her mind went numb. She couldn't even think of any prayers to say.

Miroff was miserable. Every muffled sob from the brave, young girl clawed at his heart. But, it was his duty to see this business through to the end. He had no choice. War, cold or hot, was a tragic thing and loss was inevitable. Miroff had long ago come to expect death, including his own. Still, he mourned for this beautiful child. He glared at Von Kepler, hating the Nazi.

"What now, Doctor?" Miroff demanded.

"Now, we wait," Von Kepler declared. "We wait for him to come to us – or rather, to me."

"Then what?"

"Then, I will deal with him," the German replied coolly. "With this." He pulled what looked to be an ordinary hand grenade from the pocket of his trench coat.

Miroff looked skeptical. "I thought we wanted the beast alive?"

"I do," Von Kepler proclaimed. "This is a special type of grenade that I devised myself. When it explodes, it will release microscopic particles of cadmium dust into the air that, when he inhales them, will neutralize the nuclear reaction in the creature's body and render him dormant. Then, he can be extracted from the cave at my convenience."

Von Kepler produced another object from his coat pocket – a small, rubber gas mask. "This mask will protect me from the cadmium particles, which are poisonous to the human system."

Miroff glared. "What of the girl?" he demanded. "You promised her she wouldn't be harmed if she cooperated! And where is *my* mask, Doctor?"

Von Kepler shrugged. "I lied," he said casually. "And you won't need a mask, comrade." Without warning, Von Kepler drew a German Luger from his coat pocket and aimed it at the big Russian.

Miroff went for his own pistol, but he wasn't fast enough. Von Kepler squeezed off two quick shots. The Russian groaned as he felt the bullets bury themselves in his chest and drive him back toward the precipice.

Miroff gave Betty Jo one last mournful glance as blood oozed from his grievous wounds, and then toppled over the precipice with a final growl of protest into the churning, black water below.

"I dislike sentimental henchmen," Von Kepler observed calmly. "They cannot be trusted. I can always tell his superiors at the Kremlin that he was killed by the monster."

Seeing a man cold bloodedly murdered right in front of her proved to be too much for Betty Jo. She threw back her blonde head and unleashed an anguished, high-pitched, feminine shriek that echoed throughout the big cave even more loudly than the Nazi's gunshots.

Von Kepler chuckled and aimed the Luger at Betty Jo. "That's it, my little beauty, scream! Scream your pretty head off! Draw my creation out of hiding for me."

The German fired another round, which missed Betty Jo's head by inches and shattered the rock behind her, showering her face with biting shards of debris and deafening her.

The teenager screamed again and again as each bullet slammed into the cave formation near her face, her mind besieged by terror.

Von Kepler cackled maniacally as he fired one round after another to induce the horrified girl to scream. "Scream, girl! Scream, I tell you! Scream until your lungs burst!"

Deeper in the cave, the bats fluttered to life in a fury of flapping wings, their mean little shrieks adding to the cacophony caused by the Nazi's gunfire and the teenager's screaming.

Another creature stirred from slumber as well – the atomic monster! He rose up suddenly from where he was sprawled, wolfish ears perked up at the sounds of the gunshots and the shrill, anguished screams.

He was confused, at first, and looked this way and that, trying to ascertain where the hullaballoo was coming from. In the hollow, echoing cave, sound was distorted when coming from any distance away, and even with the mutant beast's radar-like ears, it was difficult to pinpoint the source and direction of the distress.

Eventually, however, as more shots and more screams rang out, the monster's ears were able to zero in on the sounds. The radioactive behemoth belted out a terrific roar that shook the cavern walls, doubled his huge paws into fists, and bounded through the cave like a locomotive, bearing down on the sounds and on the foolhardy invaders who dared to disturb his slumber.

Professor Willoughby brought the troop carrier to a halt a few yards behind Von Kepler's green Buick and shut off the motor.

"That must be Von Kepler's car up there," the professor declared. "The brigand has a big head start on us. We mustn't lose any more time."

The old man pulled out Petrovich's gun and checked the clip for bullets. It was full. He looked gravely at the two boys. "All right, lads, this is it," he said quietly. "Remember – stout hearts. We can't afford to bungle this. Understand?"

Skip swallowed a golf ball-sized lump of fright that had swollen in his throat and managed a voiceless nod.

Johnny nodded briskly, afraid, but in control and anxious to rescue his sister.

"Very well," said the professor. "Let's get at it, then."

The three would-be heroes piled out of the troop carrier quickly. The professor turned on his big flashlight, gestured for the boys to follow him, then started off down the dusty, winding trail that led eventually to the old quarry pit.

Von Kepler laughed raucously as he peeled off two more shots, and brandished his cadmium grenade like a toy.

Betty Jo screamed again as the bullets ricocheted off of the rock formation and showered her face with cutting debris. Her cheeks were pink, swollen and bloody and her ears were ringing like bells. She could barely hear her own shrill screams as she belted them out, one after another.

The teenager's mind was in free-fall. Any second, Von Kepler might make a kill shot and bring her short life to an end. So far, he had chosen merely to toy with her, to torture her with every near miss. It was a cruel game to the demented Nazi, but a game, Betty Jo knew, with a deadly purpose.

Von Kepler's maniacal cackling came to an abrupt halt, as did his gunfire, when a great, bestial roar echoed throughout the cavern. The German paused and stared off in the direction of the sound.

Betty Jo, too, went quiet. The echo of her screams faded away. She stared through teary eyes into the darkness, her ears still ringing and useless and her throat swollen and sore.

She saw a massive shadow lurking on the cavern wall across from her – a hulking, monstrous shape lumbering from a side tunnel toward the chamber they occupied. It was the creature she had encountered on the canyon road. She knew that at once, and her heart nearly stopped beating. He was coming!

Before her, Von Kepler waited with bated breath, his goggled eyes straining in the dim light cast by the luminous algae. Then, he saw the shadow, too, and heard the great, thunderous pounding of the monster's footsteps on the stone cave floor.

Finally, he saw the brute himself – the huge mass of iron-hard flesh, clad in the gray, tattered remnants of a radiation suit, as he stomped out of a connecting tunnel and loomed there, his vast shadow cast against the cave wall behind him.

The beast looked from Von Kepler to the girl and back again, clearly trying to ascertain what was happening in his domain.

"So, there you are, my boy," the Nazi muttered. "I knew I'd find you again. It was destiny!"

The atomic monster gave an angry growl. He recognized the little yellow-haired girl cruelly bound to the cave formation at once. It was the same girl he had rescued from the fiery wreck earlier that evening. But, why was she here in his cave? Why was she fastened to that pillar? And who was this other wicked, hairless creature – the tall one with the empty, black eyes and the strange, chemical smell?

That ugly, thin-faced figure looked vaguely familiar to the monster. He stepped forward and tipped his gargoyle head curiously. Where had he seen and smelled this creature before? Was it at the Bad Place? The mutant behemoth couldn't quite recall.

"Don't you know me, boy?" Von Kepler coaxed. "Can't you recognize your creator? Do you not recall who it was who gave you back your life when you came to me, comatose and paralyzed?"

The monster closed his cat's eyes and staggered back, raising a clawed hand to his head. A flash of memory flooded into his primitive brain. It was a memory of waking up, unable to move, or make a sound. A memory of seeing a face and hearing a voice, images that were hazy and indistinct at first, but cleared presently and burned into the creature's brain.

It had been this thin, cadaverous man who had loomed over him at the Bad Place – sometimes wearing a white lab smock, sometimes in a gray, hooded suit, like the one the monster himself wore. He had peered down at him through a glass visor in the gray hood. It was those same goggled eyes, that same sharp nose, that same clipped, accented voice. He recalled hating that odious figure and knowing that he was an enemy.

Now, here he was again, with his thin, cold smile and hairless visage, still an enemy, and also an enemy of the yellow-haired girl. The angry mutant snarled in rage and lumbered forward, great claws reaching out to crush this gangly foe before he could do any more harm.

But, Von Kepler was ready for this reaction. He raised his Luger and fired another round at Betty Jo's head.

The girl screamed as the bullet ricocheted off the rock near her face.

The monster saw this and halted his advance. He crouched, tiger-like, and studied his adversary, a deep growl lodged in his throat.

Von Kepler grinned, pleased. "Ah, you are smarter than I first supposed," he observed. "The bullets, you know, are harmless to you, but they can kill the little girl. And you don't want that, do you, my boy?"

The mutant merely crouched nearby, snarling like an angry dog. He studied his enemy closely, looking for a weakness, a chance to spring!

The moon was already waning in the sky over Brush Canyon by the time Professor Willoughby and the two boys reached the ravine, scampered down it, and arrived at the mouth of Ghost Rock Cave. They lingered there only a moment to catch their breath.

The professor pulled the Russian's confiscated pistol from his coat pocket and held it ready. "We're here," the old man announced breathlessly. "This is it, lads. The moment of truth. We dare not fail in our task, or there will be dire consequences, not only for Miss Carlson, but perhaps the whole world!"

The boys exchanged a fearful glance.

"Once Von Kepler has the monster in his power," the professor continued, "there'll be no reason for him to keep Miss Carlson alive. Now, come. We're in a race against time and every second is precious!"

With that, the three of them plunged through the mouth of the cave into the black tunnel beyond, following the bright beam of the professor's powerful flashlight.

It was a stalemate, the monster quickly realized. The fiend with the gun had him at bay and he knew it.

If he charged the thin man, he would shoot the girl. The mutant knew that he wasn't fast enough to prevent it. He had no choice but to hang back and wait for an opening.

It worried the beast that the bald man didn't seem to be afraid of him. All the other humans he had encountered feared him, even the yellow-haired girl. The old man was the one exception. But, the old man was a friend, this bald man was not.

There was something else, as well. The bald man held another object in addition to the gun, a small, roundish, black item that the monster didn't recognize. The gun, the creature knew, could do him no harm. He had been shot many times, to no avail. The bullets just bounced off of his steely body.

But, this round object was something different. Perhaps, the beast mused, it could harm him. Maybe that was why the bald man showed no fear of him. The monster kept well back, watching his enemy's moves very closely.

"Are you confused, my boy?" Von Kepler goaded. "Or is your mind simply too primitive to make the connection? I am, for lack of a more accurate definition, your father." The Nazi grinned. "Yes, like Herr Frankenstein, I gave you life. You belong to me. And, as it happens, I have need of you."

The monster cocked his head curiously. He didn't fully understand the bald man's words, but he didn't like the sly, malicious tone in his voice as he spoke.

"You, my boy, or more accurately, your mutant cells, shall produce for me a new serum," Von Kepler went on. "One with which I will, at last, produce usable mutations – super *men* instead of super beasts. These supermen will exist only to obey my orders, and will fulfill the dream of Herr Hitler once and for all!"

Von Kepler's cold smile widened. "I shall breed an army of such supermen – an army that will march on every city in the world and, at last, give birth to the *New Reich*!" The mad Nazi unleashed a peel of wild, hysterical laughter that echoed throughout the entire cave.

But, at that very moment, Professor Willoughby and the two boys rushed into the cavern and quickly appraised the situation. The professor raised his stolen gun. "Drop those weapons, Heinrich! I have a pistol aimed!"

"Professor!" Betty Jo shrieked in delight.

Von Kepler whirled in bewilderment. "*You*!" he shouted in disbelief.

The old man leveled his gun on the Nazi. "Drop those weapons, Heinrich, or I swear by all that's sacred, I'll put a bullet through you!"

Von Kepler trained his Luger back on Betty Jo. "Get back, you fools, or I'll kill the girl!"

"It's over, Heinrich," the professor declared. "We've dealt with that communist hoodlum you left to guard us. And since the other one isn't here, I presume you've already killed him. There's no one left to help you. You're beaten, Heinrich."

"*Never!*" Von Kepler screamed. "We will never be beaten by you, Englander! You thought you had beaten us after the war, but here I stand, unbowed! The New Reich shall sweep over the earth like a flood!"

"Hitler is dead, and with him, so is his mad dream," the professor said flatly. "All you're doing, Heinrich, is living a dead man's twisted fantasy. The time has come for you to pay for your crimes."

Von Kepler snarled in rage like a caged animal. "You forget, Alfred! It is I who hold the last card!" He aimed the Luger at Betty Jo's ample breast and squeezed the trigger.

But, the gun only clicked. He had already used up all the bullets.

A look of horror spread over the German's face as he realized he had just bungled his last hand. Frantically, he reached for the pin in the cadmium grenade, but he was too late.

The monster saw his chance and he took it, lunging with surprising speed for so bulky a creature. He swept the grenade from Von Kepler's grasp with one swat, and then scooped the Nazi up with his other claw.

The German let out a shriek of horror as the steely talons gripped his gangly body and hoisted him high.

The monster, a deep, rumbling growl lingering in his throat, held the screaming, thrashing Nazi over his head and lumbered toward the precipice overlooking the rushing underground river.

"*Nein*!" Von Kepler shrieked out over and over in a high-pitched whine. He kicked and flailed his skinny limbs uselessly, but he was like a rag doll in the iron grip of the mutant behemoth.

Betty Jo screamed in horror and turned her face away quickly.

The professor dashed forward. "*No, Morgan!*" he shouted, waving his outstretched hands frantically. "Don't do it, lad*! Don't!*"

But, the atomic monster was having none of it. He approached the edge of the precipice and peered down at the icy, raging river below. He would put an end to this cursed enemy once and for all!

He poised himself over the precipice, ready to hurl the shrieking German to his doom, when he heard a desperate plea from the yellow-haired girl. He paused and looked back at her.

Betty Jo, still fastened to the cave pillar, looked back at the hesitant creature and pleaded with him.

"Christopher, please stop!" Betty Jo shouted. "You don't want to do this! You're not a killer, like Von Kepler. You may *look* like a monster, but you don't have to *behave* like one. Don't let him, or *anyone*, make you into something you're not."

The radioactive behemoth paused. Gradually, the fury faded from his fiery, feline eyes, and his steely limbs loosened. He gave a final look at the rushing river below, then, slowly stepped away from the precipice. He lowered the quaking Nazi to the cave floor and released him.

Von Kepler stood, quavering, whimpering like a terrified child – a waste of a man.

Professor Willoughby moved forward and patted the huge beast's bulging arm. "That's a good lad, Morgan. Good fellow, indeed."

Betty Jo smiled happily. "Thank you, Christopher. Thank you."

Skip and Johnny hurried over to release Betty Jo. Johnny produced his camp knife and began to saw on the ropes, while Skip took hold of the girl's shoulders to steady her.

"You okay?" Skip asked.

Betty Jo nodded wearily. "I think so."

A moment later, Johnny had sawed through the hemp and was tossing the rope away. Then, he and Skip led Betty Jo away from the pillar.

Von Kepler had recovered from the shock of his ordeal. Already, the hatred was boiling up inside him. As his four enemies commiserated nearby, the German delved into his coat pocket and withdrew the switchblade – determined to destroy at least one of his hated adversaries.

He selected Professor Willoughby, the one he hated most of all. He pressed the button on the hilt of the knife and the deadly blade flashed out with a click.

"Die, you old swine!" the Nazi shrieked as he lunged toward the professor. "*Die!*"

The monster stepped forward, seized the German before he'd reached his goal, and hurled him backwards while the professor and the others shrank away.

Von Kepler stumbled back to the edge of the precipice and there lost his balance and tumbled backwards.

"Nein!" he screamed as he toppled over the edge. "*Nein!*"

But, there was no stopping his descent. He plummeted, shrieking and flailing, down into the icy, black torrent below and hit the water with a tumultuous splash.

Von Kepler surfaced only once as the racing current swept his thrashing body away. Then, with one last defiant shriek, the Nazi was sucked under and disappeared. Even his dislodged hat was swept away into the impenetrable darkness.

Betty Jo had screamed and buried her face in Skip's shoulder as the Nazi went over the edge. When it was all over, she looked up. The last of the German's echoing shrieks had ebbed away down the dark tunnel.

Betty Jo glanced up at Skip. He smiled down at her and pressed her small body against his comfortingly. Just this once, Betty Jo allowed him to hold her, as she knew he'd always wished to. She needed it.

Johnny approached the professor and took hold of the old man's coat tail. He swallowed, a little shocked. "Golly, he drowned, Professor..."

"Yes," the old man said quietly.

Still hand in hand, Betty Jo and Skip joined the others at the edge of the precipice and stared down into the icy torrent below.

"What a horrid way to die," Betty Jo remarked in a hollow voice.

"Better than he deserved, the scoundrel!" the professor commented darkly.

Betty Jo glanced over at the mutant goliath, who stood a few feet away from them, regarding them curiously with his large, catlike eyes.

"What about him?" she asked, a little sadly. "What about poor Christopher? What's to become of him?"

The professor laid a hand on Betty Jo's shoulder. "I don't know, my dear," he admitted wearily. "But, one thing I'm certain of – whatever fate has in store for the poor brute, as long as he has friends like the three of you, he won't have to endure it alone."

Betty Jo smiled, happy for the first time all night. "Right," she confirmed.

For his part, the atomic monster was happy too. He looked over his new friends approvingly. At least now, he would no longer be lonely. Here were three more, aside from the old man, who would not run away screaming when they saw him coming. These were friends, and friends were precious things to have – especially for a monster.

But, it was night, now, and his new friends were weary and sore. Even the beast could see that. There would be plenty of time to get to know them another day. He knew that now, and it was a very comforting thing to know.

With a satisfied grunt, the mutant goliath turned and lumbered back into the deeper recesses of the cave, beyond the dim glow of the luminous algae, into the night-black darkness of the great tunnel. The evil cloud that hung over him, the horrid, patchy memories of the Bad Place and of the time before it, gradually faded from the beast's simple brain. That dark time was over and a new day was dawning. A new day full of promise and, just perhaps, full of happiness as well.

The four humans watched and waved until the hulking brute disappeared into the darkness of the tunnel. When he'd gone, the professor turned to the three kids and smiled warmly.

"Well, I think we've all had more than enough excitement for one evening," the old man said wearily. "We'd best get Miss Carlson and young Johnny home and to bed."

Betty Jo reached down, scooped up her exhausted little brother, and rested him gently on her hip. "Professor," she said tiredly, "that's the best suggestion I've heard all evening."

Epilogue

Professor Willoughby stood in front of Colonel Morris Fielding's desk, waiting as the colonel read through the report the old man had prepared for the third time.

After a moment, the colonel laid the report aside, sighed deeply, and then regarded the peculiar, archaic-looking old gentleman who hovered over his desk.

"Let me get this straight, Professor," the colonel said finally. "You say that Von Kepler, and the creature he created at Project Omega, both went over that ledge together and drowned in the underground river?"

"For the umpteenth time, yes," the old man replied. "It's all there in the report I prepared for the State Department. The one you've just read for the third time. Why it was necessary to drag me all the way here to the Pentagon to make a direct report, I'm at a loss to understand."

The colonel laced his fingers together and gave the professor an appraising glance. He was usually a shrewd judge of character, and something told him not to trust the old Englishman completely.

"Because, you ran out on us at Project Omega before completing your assignment there, Professor," the colonel declared. "Not only that, you stole government property – namely a troop carrier, which you still haven't accounted for. You bucked the Brass during the war, and you're still bucking us now. I can honestly say that I don't fully trust you."

The professor grinned sardonically. "Wise foreign policy," he observed.

Colonel Fielding narrowed his eyes. "Who's side are you really on?" he demanded.

"My own, of course," the professor declared without hesitation. He abruptly seated himself across from the colonel.

"Look, Fielding," he began as he packed his pipe with tobacco, "that Marine sub-aqua team you sent to Brush Canyon searched the river. And the squad they came with combed the canyon for a week. They found nothing. Why are you still digging?"

The colonel stood up and crossed to his office window, which overlooked the Pentagon grounds.

Outside, a soft summer rain was coming down, leaving its traces on the glass. The colonel bore a troubled frown on his stony face. Years of military service and two wars had made him a cautious man.

"Because, I smell a rat," he declared. "You left things out of that report, and I know it. Like how the Russians got in on the act. How did they even know about Project Omega?"

The professor shrugged. "That should be easy enough for even you to understand," he pointed out. "After Von Kepler escaped, he knew his project was doomed. He was now a hunted man. I believe he'd planned for that eventuality and had been hedging his bet all along."

"By selling information to the Russians?"

"Among others," the professor answered. "He might've been hooked up with Bund factions, as well. Maybe even the Chinese. Where the money to fund his madness came from wouldn't have mattered to Von Kepler."

The colonel nodded. "That much, I'll buy," he said.

"Did you squeeze anything out of that KGB hooligan we handed you?" the professor asked.

"Not much," the colonel admitted. "He managed to slip himself a cyanide capsule during the interrogation. He was dead before he hit the floor."

"Good riddance," the professor observed.

"Agreed," said Colonel Fielding. "But, that leaves us high and dry." He came back to his desk and sat down. He ran his hand through his thinning, gray hair. "We're as in the dark as ever on this thing. We don't even know just how much that Kraut told the Ruskies."

"As little as possible," Professor Willoughby replied. "Von Kepler was in business strictly for himself, I assure you."

"I'll buy that, too," said the colonel.

The professor spread his hands wide. "Then, why all the mystery?" he asked. "It all seems fairly cut-and-dried to me, Fielding."

The colonel raised a finger to object, but quickly thought better of it. Instead, he lit himself a cigarette and eased back in his chair.

"I don't like loose ends," he said at last. "They come back up like bad food. If the Commies know too much, they could use it to clobber us politically. The world is already teetering back and forth, and it wouldn't take much to tilt it the wrong way."

The professor raised a bushy brow. "It seems to me *both* ways leave a lot to be desired," he pointed out wryly.

The colonel cut the old man a wicked glance. "That's why I don't trust you, Willoughby," he grumbled. "You're too damn flip for my taste. Don't forget that you're still a guest in this country, and unless you'd like to hop a boat back to jolly, old England, you'd better learn to play by our rules."

The professor stood up, his patience at an end. He pocketed his pipe. "No need to get nervous, Fielding," he lectured. "Your dirty little secret is safe. Von Kepler and the poor creature are dead. The Russian agents are both dead. And everyone else involved has been sworn to secrecy. You can go to bed tonight with a clean slate. Clean on the surface, that is."

Fielding straightened. "What did you mean by that crack?" he demanded.

The professor donned his frock coat and tweed cap. "You know perfectly well what I meant," he declared. "You Yanks like to pass around the fairy story that you have a paradise here in the colonies. But, we both know there's a stain on your white hat."

The professor headed for the office door, pausing there for a moment to make one last observation. "There's a dark side to *your* paradise."

The old man gave a nod of farewell and then went out the door.

Colonel Fielding sat sullenly in his chair, puffing on his cigarette, a grim, sour expression marring his granite face. After a moment of reflection, he gathered up the Project Omega Report and held it out over his newly emptied metal waste basket.

He produced a Zippo cigarette lighter from his jacket pocket, lit the bottom corner of the report, and watched it slowly burn in his fingers before he finally dropped it into the waste basket.

As the black smoke billowed up from the waste basket, Colonel Fielding eased back in his chair – not exactly at peace, but, at least, a little calmer than he had been for the last three months. The specter of Project Omega had haunted him the whole time, and now, all that remained of that nightmare was a pile of ashes at the bottom of his trash can. At least, he hoped so.

Outside, crossing the Pentagon grounds, his umbrella raised against the cool, Washington D.C. drizzle, Professor Willoughby made his way to the nearest bus stop.

He was eager to be on the first plane back to California. His lies fooled the Pentagon Brass. They bought the story that both Von Kepler, and his monster, had drowned in the underground river.

Now the creature, the Beast of Brush Canyon, the Unthinkable Hybrid, would be safe – for the time being at any rate. So would the professor's three young confederates. All that remained now was to keep the secret for as long as possible.

The Unthinkable Hybrid

By the time the professor reached the bus stop, the early summer drizzle had ceased and the sun was peeking through the thinning clouds above. Its golden rays felt warm and refreshing on the old man's plump face.

As the bus pulled up and the professor stepped aboard, the bus driver smiled at him. "Welcome aboard, sir," he said pleasantly. He glanced out the window at the sunny sky above. "Well," he observed. "The rain's stopped. It looks like it's gonna be a nice day after all."

Professor Willoughby paused by the driver and smiled widely. "Yes," he agreed. "I believe it's going to be a wonderful day. A wonderful day, indeed."

Author's note

Thanks very much for reading, folks. I hope you enjoyed the story. With any luck, there will be plenty more stories to tell about the atomic monster and his friends. But, before all of that ensues, I feel it's appropriate to explain a little about the history of *The Unthinkable Hybrid.*

Way back in the mid-1980s, after watching a monster movie from the 1950s, I had the idea of writing a story, or screenplay, about a 1950s-type monster. At the time, I didn't want to set it in the '50s, just give it the feel of the period. Unfortunately, that idea never seemed to work. I kept fiddling with it for three decades, changing the characters, the story elements, etc. But, no matter what I did, it never quite worked.

Finally, after watching a marathon of '50s monster movies in December of 2008, I realized that the only way I could get my idea to work right was to set it in the period which inspired it – the 1950s.

After that, everything fell into place just like Dominoes. I had the right story, the right characters, and, most importantly, the right *monster.*

I wrote the first draft in June of 2009. I even drew up a comic book version of the first act, which I printed with *Kablam.* I sent queries to dozens of agents and publishers, but none were interested. I had only one official rejection letter from an agent, and he called the material "utterly ridiculous". But, I didn't give up on the idea.

When the book failed to find a publisher, I turned back to the comic book idea, this time truncating the book into a two issue comic, which I then put up as a webcomic on two different webcomic sites. The webcomic version ran for three years total and eleven issues before the tragic death of my mother caused me to stop posting it.

Three years later, I decided to revive my dormant monster and do a print comic version. I drew all new images and was in the process of doing the computer color work when I realized that the time involved in doing a comic book wasn't cost effective. It was at that point I decided to turn it back into a print book.

Instead of returning to the good, but overly long original book, I wrote a new version based on the webcomic adaption. This is the version you have just read. It's a more condensed version, but more readable as well.

I hope to continue the stories well into the future with a whole series of print books chronicling the adventures of 'Hybie', as his webcomic fans called him, and his human friends. I hope all of you will come along for the ride.

Thanks again.

About the Author

Vincent F. Wyler is a self-proclaimed "amateur everything" who dabbles in art of almost every kind. He describes himself as a "Pot-bellied, balding, middle-aged hack with archaic tastes and a bad temper." He lives in Illinois with his pet tortoise, Henrietta.